THE
BLOODLETTERS

SAMANTHA BELL

THE
BLOODLETTERS

SAMANTHA BELL

ONE

THE DAY AFTER MY MOTHER'S FUNERAL, THEY CAME FOR ME.

I was sitting in my private room by the window that looked over the gardens. It was springtime; the flowers were blooming in a riot of colors. I watched birds flit around from tree to tree and the breeze ruffle the leaves slowly.

I heard footsteps outside my door. I quickly snapped my eyes back to the history book that I should be studying. As a Minister's daughter, it was expected of me to know the history of our kingdom in fine detail.

"When the war was over and Inwaed was founded, the top warriors emerged as kings, blessed by the Gods with longevity, beauty, and strength in exchange for

1

the blood they must consume," I whispered, knowing this passage by heart. I ran my fingers over the wrinkled paper.

The footsteps paused by my door and then continued down the hall. I waited until the echo of heels vanished before exhaling and closing the heavy tome on my lap. I stretched my arms and glanced back out the window.

My younger brothers, Charles, and Samuel were walking towards the stables. They must have finished their lessons early. I frowned, watching their blond hair glint in the sunlight. They dressed in matching breeches with their helmets dangling carelessly in their hands. Charles was swinging a riding crop while Samuel, the younger of the pair, laughed.

I shook my head and left my window seat. I set the history book on my desk and paused at my mirror. Every time I looked at myself, I saw my mother. I had her same tall and slender build, same blue eyes, and same freckled skin. My hair was lighter than hers, the color of the amber ring she always wore.

I glanced at the photo slipped into the frame of the mirror. My mother, Lady Sophia Ackerman, dressed in finery, the night of my father's election. That was twelve years ago. I had just turned five. My only memories of that night were how boring the ceremony was and how lovely my mother looked in green silk.

I clenched my fists and turned away. Hot tears stung my eyes, and I wiped them away furiously. I swore to myself I was done crying since her funeral yesterday. I hated mourning, but what I hated most was that I seemed to be the only one stricken by her sudden illness and passing.

My father, Lord Henry Ackerman, had a face like a stone wall. As the Minister of the city, he was too busy to be with my mother in her time of need. He was always too busy for everything, immersing himself in politics. Avoiding his family. Avoiding me more than all of them put together.

I was his eldest child; my mother had named me Violet. The doctors said it was a miracle the day I was born. It had been a complicated pregnancy, and I was purple and still when I came into this world. My mother's song had brought the first cry from my lips; she had resurrected me from the dead.

I ran my fingers through my loose curly hair and tied it back into a bun at the base of my neck. Though it was my imagination, I could have sworn I heard my tutor's voice in my head, reminding me of my studies. I rolled my eyes, glaring at the pile of books about politics and history. I loved to read, but the dry contents of these texts made me want to burn every single last one of them.

I was the heir to the Ackerman family. As my father's eldest child, I would one day take the title of Minister from him, unless a non-confidence election was called or if the Royals intervened. My father was young, only thirty-three when he won the election twelve years ago. The Ackerman's had always been an influential family. It was no surprise that when my father ran for office of Wythtir that he won by a landslide. The Ministry system was straight-forward: once the people elected a minster, his family would rule until they were determined to be unfit. The minister who ruled before my father's election had died without an heir, so the Royals called an election. It was the first in several generations. Some provinces had a high turnover; others had been in the same family since the time of the wars.

Sometimes I wondered what life would have been like if he hadn't won the election if we had just continued our simple but luxurious lives with the rest of the upper class. Maybe I would have had friends or a fiancé. Now I was being simultaneously groomed by tutors and councilors while being looked down upon by my father.

I smoothed the wrinkles out of my blouse and summoned the strength to return to my studies. After lunch, maybe I would go riding and forget about the world for a while.

There was a knock at the door. A quick rap that I recognized as Mrs. Barber, one of our housekeepers.

"Come in," I called.

"Miss Violet, dear, lunch will be ready momentarily." Mrs. Barber was a short, portly woman. She had been our housekeeper before my father's election. My mother insisted that she come with us since she was a widow and her husband's meager pension would have forced her on the streets.

I checked the clock on the wall. The gilded hands pointed up; it was nearly noon. Where had the morning gone? Wasted away in reading dusty books and memorizing facts that my father himself probably didn't know.

"Oh, thank you, Mrs. Barber," I said with a smile. As soon as lunch was over, I would be free to enjoy the afternoon.

"Lord Ackerman is taking lunch on the terrace," Mrs. Barber continued. "He has requested that you join him."

I didn't hide the groan from the housekeeper. I hadn't seen my father since the funeral, and there I only posed for photos and avoided looking at him while I spoke my part of the eulogy.

Mrs. Barber gave me a patient look. "Now dear, you must know that your mother's passing has been difficult on all of us. Perhaps Lord Ackerman most of all. You know he loved your mother."

My grandmothers had both passed when I was young, and I considered Mrs. Barber to be part of our family. I looked away from her, trying not to notice that her eyes had gone misty. My father had never been open with his emotions; my mother always said it was because of his position. He couldn't how weakness and risk raising the suspicions of the people—or worse, the Royals.

5

I forced a smile and sighed. "I supposed you're right," I conceded. The clock on the wall chimed, marking the noon hour.

Mrs. Barber gave me a nod and left without another word.

I checked myself in the mirror once more and then made my way to the third-floor terrace. The Minister's Manor was large, more than twice the size of the townhome which I had spent my first five years. It was three stories high, with countless bedrooms, bathrooms, offices and a small ballroom for entertaining guests. We employed about a dozen servants, including Mrs. Barber, who kept the house, the grounds and our family in impeccable condition.

I walked past our small library, remembering the party last month where I had stolen away with Councilor Wentworth's son. He had told me it was his intention to court me formally if our fathers would approve it. I grimaced at being betrothed to such a clumsy lover. Thankfully, his champagne-driven promises were never formalized.

The terrace was near my father's office and smaller than the one on the ground floor where we would host receptions and parties. The doors were open, letting in a gentle breeze. I could hear the clinking of plates and silverware as a servant set the table.

My father sat at the table, reading the daily newspaper. The crest of the province of Wythtir, the province he was Minister of, was embroidered on the lapel of his black jacket. He wore black from head to toe. It was custom for a widower to mourn for seventy days following the death of his wife. Today was day number ten; I knew because I had counted them.

My father looked up, hearing my footsteps on the stone. "Ah, Violet, there you are." He folded his newspaper on his lap. His eyes rimmed red as if he had also been crying recently.

I held my head high and sat across from him. "Father," I said curtly.

The servant set down a shallow bowl of leek soup in front of me. There was a plate of thin cheese sandwiches between us. He filled my glass with white wine and then tended to my father. I didn't take a bite, waiting for my father to speak. He had a look in his eyes; he was thinking about something. It was a look that his political adversaries never seemed to notice, but I caught it easily.

Lord Ackerman didn't meet my gaze. Instead, he busied himself with his soup.

"Will Charles and Samuel be joining us today?" I said. I knew full well that they were in the stables but forced conversation was better than his infuriating slurping.

My father looked up. "Ah, no, my dear. I hoped that we could spend some time together today."

"I see," I replied. I took a sip of wine before continuing. "And why would that be, Father?"

The Minister looked flustered at my question. "What do you mean? Surely a father can enjoy a meal with his daughter. With his heir." He added.

I narrowed my eyes but quickly masked my suspicion. My father had never taken an interest in me. He coached me through tutors, avoided me at family gatherings, and made it no secret that he favored his sons over me.

I knew why, of course, but he had no idea. My mother and I were always close; I was her only daughter, after all. Shortly after her diagnosis, she admitted to me that she had an affair around the time I was conceived. Father had always believed that I was a bastard, not a child of his blood. With me looking exactly like my mother, there wasn't proof aside from my mother's word.

"You must be the perfect heir." Mother said to me that night. "Prove to him that you can be a great ruler, a smart politician, and he will come to love you."

I knew now that I didn't want his love and I would have gladly traded his life for hers.

"I know that your mother's passing has been hard," my father continued. "But we must carry on, for her sake." He paused, looking me in the eye for the first time since I sat down. "You look just like her, you know."

I knew. I heard it all the time, but I had never heard it from him. "Yes," I agreed, busying myself with a sandwich.

The breeze ruffled the tablecloth and pulled tendrils of my amber colored hair out of the bun. When the servant came to refill my drink, I gladly let him and then let the silence settle upon us. I glanced back at my father, who was staring out towards the gardens.

I pushed the soup away and folded my napkin. "Well, thank you for lunch, Father," I said briskly. "I think I shall be going now." I stood.

"Are you going to go out for a ride?" Lord Ackerman asked, not commenting that I had barely eaten a bite.

"Yes, I think I shall," I replied and quickly left the terrace.

I wondered why he had taken such a sudden interest in me. I shook my head. My father had always hated me, even if he had never said it outright. I rolled my shoulders and pushed away the anxious thoughts. He was in mourning; people always did strange things when they were upset. But I forced myself to go forward. I loved my mother dearly; she was the only one in our family that I could connect with – but she was gone. No amount of tears would bring her back. If I would be a Minister one day, I couldn't let anything hold me down.

I dressed in black riding breeches and a matching jacket. While it was socially appropriate for me to wear color after the funeral, I couldn't bring myself to wear my favorite red riding clothes. I pulled on my leather boots and made my way down to the stables without incident.

The musky smell of leather and hay met me when I pushed opened the heavy doors. Mr. Finnegan, the stable hand was tending to a mare and her young foal. He nodded towards me and smiled. "Good afternoon, Mr. Finnegan."

"Afternoon, Miss Violet," he replied. "Are you going for a ride? Can I help you with anything?"

I shook my head. "No, thank you. I'm sure Lily needs you more needs you more than me."

The stable hand grinned and patted the gray mare's neck. "Alright, miss, but call if you need something, alright?"

I nodded and walked down the aisle to where my mare was in her stall. She arched her neck over the boards and snorted. I rubbed her velvety nose before pushing open the door and taking her by her halter. She was a patient horse that my father had bought me when I was twelve. In the five years I had ridden her we knew each other so well it took no time for her headgear and saddle.

I met my brothers as I left the stable. Their horses were sweaty and frothing at the mouth. They greeted me with sneers.

"All done studying, Violet?" Samuel said.

Charles dismounted and threw the reins into Mr. Finnegan's waiting hands.

Samuel did the same and pulled off his helmet, shaking his blond hair.

While I looked like my mother, both of my brothers took after my father. Their eyes were the same dark green, the same square jaws and broad builds.

"What about your studies?" I turned their question back on them, absentmindedly twisting my mare's mane through my fingers.

Charles snorted. "Finished. Going to eat." Samuel nodded.

Mr. Finnegan took their horses without a word.

"You know, you could wash your own horses," I said.

"Yeah, right! That's what servants are for," Charles said.

I clenched my teeth. Both of my brothers were so young when my father won the election, they couldn't remember a time where they weren't waited on hand and foot. "Well, when I left, I was sure that I smelled apple tarts being baked in the kitchen."

My brothers looked at each other and dashed off in the manor's direction.

I rolled my eyes. That always worked on them and Mrs. Barber would wrangle them into doing some chores before getting their prize. As spoiled as they were, no one ever said no to that woman – except maybe my father.

I shook the thoughts of my family away and mounted my mare. I named her Firefly when I was a girl, a name that seemed silly next to Charles and Samuel's Maximus and Titan, respectively. I patted Firefly's neck and clicked my tongue. "Come on, girl, let's ride."

I guided her towards the large riding arena. We picked up speed, and she cleared the metal gate with ease. I lost myself and my worries for hours.

I rode until teatime. Then, after washing Firefly and saying a quick goodbye to Mr. Finnegan, I returned to my room to change.

My black blouse and skirt from the morning were already whisked away to be washed. I threw my sweaty riding gear into the hamper, washed my face, and changed into a simple black dress. I brushed my hair and tied it into a bun. These days, we were always having visitors and well-wishers coming to comfort us and I had to be presentable.

There was a knock at my door. It wasn't the familiar rhythm of Mrs. Barber or any other hand that I could recognize.

"Yes?" I called out cautiously.

"Violet, dear, it's me." My father's voice drifted under the door.

I hesitated. Seeing him twice in one day? The man that tried to pretend I didn't exist. That was even stranger than the lunch invitation.

"I'll be down in a minute, Father," I said and pushed my feet into my favorite black shoes.

"Well, actually, there's something I need to talk to you about. Privately."

My father sounded nervous. That was an emotion I had never witnessed from him before in my life. Even during important meetings, and visits from the Royals. Never had I heard his voice shake like that before. I bit my lip. "Ok," I said warily. I opened the door to see my father in his dinner jacket. There was a bead of sweat on his balding head. "Hello, Violet," he greeted with a smile.

"What did you need to speak to me about that couldn't wait until dinner?" My voice was cool, indifferent. I couldn't let him see me worry.

"Well, you see," my father said. "There won't be any dinner tonight." Two men appeared behind him. They were as wide as they were tall, dressed in suits. They looked at me with stoic expressions.

I tilted my head to look up at them and took a step back. "What do you mean?" My relaxed facade was crumbling.

The men shouldered past my father, each of them grabbing one of my arms.

I pulled against them, but their strength overcame me easily. "I don't understand!" I shrieked. "What's going on?"

My father's nervousness transformed into contempt. "My dear, now that your mother has left us," he chuckled. "Well, I don't see the need to keep you around anymore."

I pulled against my captors. The skin on my arms was turning red and blotchy. "What?" My legs trembled beneath me. Of course, he would rid himself of the child he never loved. Seeing my face would only bring him pain and anger, he never wanted me as an heir. "Let me go!" I grunted. "You can't do this; people will ask questions! You can't kill me!"

Lord Ackerman stepped back in surprise. "Kill you? No, my dear, I won't be doing that. Your mother made me promise her on her deathbed that I would take care of you *and take care of you* I shall." He snapped his fingers, and the men hauled me to a standing position again.

"You could never be my heir. Charles will do a much better job at that. Seventeen long years I've waited to get rid of you. Finally, I'll never have you see your mother's betrayal again." My father waved the men away.

The men pulled me down the hall towards the servant's entrance.

"No, please!" I stammered. "You can't do this. Father! I'm your daughter. I'm your blood!"

Lord Ackerman looked over his shoulder. "I have no daughter."

One man grabbed me by my throat and squeezed.

I gagged, seeing stars. I gasped for air and struggled. "I'll never forgive you!" I spat at my father and then everything went black.

TWO

WHEN I WOKE UP, I WAS ON A TRAIN.

I was sitting on a seat with my hands tied behind my back. With a glance around, I realized I was in a sleeper cabin and completely alone. I noticed my leather suitcase on the seat across from me. Last time I used it was during our family trip. I tried to loosen the ties around my wrists but the leather only bit into my skin. I groaned and pulled myself upright.

Through the window, I could see that the sky was dark, and the moon hung full and heavy. Trees were flying past, glowing in the moonlight. We were somewhere out in the country and moving fast, based on sounds of steam being belched out of the engine.

"Hello?" I called out.

There was a moment of quiet and then the door of the cabin unlocked and slid open. One of the men from my kidnapping was standing there, as straight-faced as before.

"Good, you're here." I put on my brisk, business-like tone. "Could you please untie me, sir?"

The man frowned.

"Please?" I continued. "You've proven that you're stronger than me and it's not like I am stupid enough to jump out of a moving train."

The man blinked. His jaw moved as he thought about my request. He took a step back and shut the door with a click.

I let out an exhausted sigh. My stomach grumbled. Judging by the position of the moon in the sky, it had been hours since the incident with my father. I clenched my teeth. He would take care of me. What did that mean? What did he have planned for me in lieu of murdering me?

My fingers tingled, and I flexed them to get the blood flowing again. What was I going to do? I couldn't try to escape with my hands like this, and I doubted I could get away from the brute outside my door even if I was untied. I cursed myself for not taking self-defence lessons like my mother had suggested. The thought of an assassination or kidnapping hadn't been a concern until tonight.

I tapped my feet, trying to think of a solution when the door clicked again. I looked up to see a woman standing there. She looked to be in her thirties with ebony skin and kinky black hair. I gasped and then remembered my manners. Foreigners were a rare sight in Inwaed.

"Good evening, Miss Ackerman." The lady said. She took a seat across from me. She was dressed well, her green skirt fell to her calves and poked out just under the hem of her navy coat. Thin gold rings decorated her long fingers.

I sat up straighter and found my polite, relaxed tone again. "Good evening." I resisted the urge to fidget with my hands.

"I must apologize for the accommodations." The woman gestured to the train cabin. Based on the scratched wood and faded upholstery, we were in coach class.

I forced an indifferent smile. "Not at all, Miss?"

"Igwe. Heather Igwe, you can call me Heather." The woman said.

I motioned to extend my hand to her and winced, forgetting for a moment about my arms being tied.

Heather gasped and stood, gently pulling me forward to see the bindings. She muttered something under her breath and produced a small knife from the pocket of her coat. She made short work of the leather straps and released my hands.

I gasped with relief and rubbed my wrists. There were bruises where the bindings had been.

Heather frowned, noting the bruises on my wrist and the ones that no doubt had bloomed on my throat. "I'm sorry," she apologized. "You were not supposed to be harmed."

"Bit late for that," I muttered.

There was a jolt as the train started to slow down. I looked out the window, catching glances of buildings I did not recognize.

"Where are we?" I asked.

The woman tilted her head and looked out the window. "The last stop before reaching the Capital, I expect."

"The Capital?" I exclaimed, jumping to my feet. "Why are we going there?"

Heather motioned for me to sit down.

The giant man outside of the cabin peeked in and frowned at me.

I glared back at him before sitting back down.

Heather waited for the door to close before speaking. "Your father has entrusted me and my colleagues to ensure you have safe travel to the Capital."

"But the Capital is only for –"

"Royals, yes, I know," Heather said.

I examined her closely. When dressed plainly, there wasn't a clear way to tell a Royal from a commoner. In stories, writers claimed that their eyes were bright, their skin shone like the moon, and had the strength of ten men. I had only seen Royals in person once in all my life, shortly after my father's election, and I knew the books were wrong. They looked the same as everyone else and that's what made them so dangerous.

Heather met my gaze. "In case you're wondering, no, I'm not a Royal."

I looked away quickly, staring at the raw skin on my wrists. "I'm sorry," I murmured. The severity of the situation was settling in as the shock melted away. My hands started to tremble. "Why would my father do this?" I breathed.

Heather was silent.

I choked back a sob and hunched over to hide my face from her. I had never shown weakness like this before. Even at my mother's funeral, my tears were restrained and elegant. It was only when I was alone that I let my true emotions show. I was exhausted, hungry, and my forehead throbbed. I wanted to wake up, surely this had to be some terrible nightmare.

The car lurched as the train came to a full stop. The whistle blew and there was a bang as a door down the aisle opened. I could hear the murmur of patrons exiting the train and I wished I was among them.

Heather sat as still as a statue.

I quickly wiped my eyes on the sleeve of my dress before sitting up to face her. I set my jaw, realizing she looked at me without pity. "Why?"

Heather opened her mouth to reply but was cut off by a shrill whistle.

A man's voice echoed down the aisle. "Attention, attention. We will now depart for the Capital. Registration is required. Any passenger without proper documentation will be forced to leave at once." Judging by the volume of his voice, the guard was only a few cabins from ours.

I forced a laugh and shrugged. "Oh whoops, in all the excitement of being kidnapped I forgot my citizen card," I said. "Guess we'll be needing to get off here."

Heather shook her head in amusement. "Nice try, Miss Violet," she said. "That's not the registration they're talking about."

A moment later, the door to our cabin slid open. The tall man was standing with another man in a navy blue uniform. He was portly, with a thick mustache and wary eyes. "Registration please."

Heather stood and nodded her head to him graciously. "Yes, sir." She reached into her pocket and withdrew a small red folder. There was a black crest stamped on the front. She presented it to the guard with both hands. "I work for Madam Desjardins. Registered Blood House number fifty-three, under license and protection of the Bloodletting Regulation Act."

The guard took the folder from her with a snap. He flipped it open and scanned over the pages quickly. "She's new, then?" He asked gruffly.

"Yes, Madam Desjardins just signed for her last night," Heather explained. "She will go for inspection

20

upon our arrival in the Capital. As you can see, all the paperwork is in order."

The guard flipped through the pages again. "And you are Ms. Igwe, I presume?" He raised a bushy eyebrow at her.

Heather nodded, flashing her citizen card.

"Alright," The guard sighed and handed the folder back to Heather.

I only realized I had been holding my breath when the door closed behind him. I gasped and all of my hopes of getting off the train vanished. "Bloodletting?" I shrieked.

Heather silenced me with a look, waiting for the guard to be far enough not to overhear. "Yes, Miss Violet." Her calm expression infuriated me. "Bloodletting," she repeated. "Your father has signed a contract with Madam Desjardins, who now has full custody of you."

I stammered, my lips trembling. "What do you mean? I'm seventeen, you can't – he can't sign my life away!"

"A seventeen-year-old is a child in the eyes of the law. Therefore, your father has every right to do what he has done. Once you become a legal adult, then the contract will be revisited." Heather's eyes flashed a warning.

I bit back my retort. I knew the laws as well as she did, probably better. I wouldn't be a legal adult until my nineteenth birthday, and I didn't like the idea of being in a contract with some strange woman for a year and a half. I clenched my fists, balling up the fabric on my lap.

Heather sighed. "I'm not your enemy, Miss Violet," she said in a softer voice. "I was your in shoes, not too long ago." She gazed out the window. The train whistled as it began to pull out of the station.

I watched her in silence. I observed her high cheekbones, her full lips and the way her hair bounced with the motion of the train. After a while, I spoke again. "What's Bloodletting?"

Heather cocked an eyebrow in my direction. "You don't know?"

I flushed. I hated admitting ignorance. "No," I blurted. "At least, it's never been mentioned in my studies or any of the books I've read." The pity in the woman's dark eyes made my cheeks blaze. No one had ever looked at me like that before.

Heather hesitated. "I see," she said finally. "I guess that's to be expected. Few of the elite find their way to Madam Desjardins' door, and never a Minister's child." She sighed. She shrugged off her coat and folded it neatly before settling back in her seat. "Well, while we have the time, I guess I'll inform you."

My mouth went dry with anticipation.

"Bloodletting is the act of giving your blood to a Royal for consumption. A Bloodletter is a person who gives their blood to the Royals."

I felt my throat close in terror. "Giving my blood?" In all my years of studying, I had never heard of these terms. I scanned my memories, trying to figure out where I could have missed it. The Royals had to drink blood to sustain themselves, that I knew, but it had never occurred to me where the blood would have come from. I shivered. "I think I'm going to be sick."

Heather continued, ignoring my outburst. "It's quite tame, I assure you. Not like the horror stories of the past. It's well regulated, controlled and monitored for the safety of the Royals, and us," she added.

"You're a Bloodletter?" I gasped. I quickly scanned her neck and arms for scars, some telltale sign of her violent lifestyle, but there were none.

Heather smiled patiently. "Yes, I am. I am the house mentor, working under Madam Desjardins. It's my job to retrieve the new members and educate them."

I looked away. "Oh," I mumbled. I brushed the tender skin on my wrists, willing myself to wake up from this nightmare. My salvation never came.

"You should rest," Heather said. She stood and tucked her folded coat under her arm. She pulled the curtains and tied them closed. "We will reach the Capital by morning."

THREE

MORNING CAME TOO SOON.

After Heather left, I curled up onto my side and sat huddled in my seat. No one came to the cabin for the rest of the trip.

The first light of dawn shone through the curtains. I rubbed my eyes. I felt exhausted but I couldn't sleep. All I could think about was how my father had betrayed me and how my life was now in the hands of Heather, Madam Desjardins, and the Royals.

I hugged my knees to my chest, ignoring my growling stomach. I scanned my memory for any knowledge about bloodletting but found none.

In the past, hundreds of years ago, when our country was new, the Royals took control. Before

Inwaed, the large island had been fought over by eight city-states, each trying to gain the most land and resources. When the tension reached its apex, all eight states engaged in a bloody war that lasted years. Finally, just when no end was in sight, the bravest, smartest, and strongest warriors from all the states joined together.

There was a call for reform, and a singular government would lead all eight states. The states became provinces of Inwaed, with the Capital in the very center. Ministers would represent the provinces and would work with the Royals to ensure that Inwaed would be a safe, prosperous and peaceful country.

The union of warriors became the Royals. The Royals were human but blessed with unbelievable strength, intelligence, beauty, and longevity. Legends said that the Gods, who craved peace for the citizens had blessed them with these supernatural gifts. The common people of Inwaed came to fear them – for their power could only be sustained by drinking blood. The history book mentioned a mandatory blood tax that was abolished about a century before I was born. There was no mention of bloodletting.

After my father's election, Royals attended the ceremony and reception. I was only a small child, but I could remember wondering what was so special about them. Why did they have power over us? They looked no different from any other human I had met. When I voiced this question to my mother, she snapped at me to never say or think about it again. The Royals were our leaders, and that was that.

I had lived with the question hovering in the back of my mind, and my studies and training offered no further explanation. I knew my place as a Minister's daughter and that one day I would be a Minister myself. Only then would I be able to interact with the Royals frequently and maybe then I would see what was so special about them.

My stomach growled again. "Would it have killed them to give their prisoner a meal?" I sighed. My body was stiff, and my headache had only intensified. I held onto the seat and forced myself to stand and stretch.

The train had slowed down again. I walked to the window and pulled back the curtains. I couldn't help but gasp.

We were in the Capital. The train tracks ran straight, with only an iron fence dividing the speeding machine from the buildings. We were cutting through a residential district, with houses packed together tightly. I could see the taller buildings of the city in the distance. They stretched up into the sky, at least six stories.

The cabin door slid open. I sat down quickly, embarrassed at my awe of the Capital. I had never seen it before, though my father went often.

Heather smiled at me. "We're here."

In the moments I was entrapped at the view, I had forgotten about my fate. Seeing Heather brought me back to the present, and I felt the dread take hold of my body again.

"Five minutes until Afonyr." The guard's voice bellowed down the hall. "Last stop Brenhinyr, expected time of arrival eight-thirty."

I glanced back out the window. I summoned all of my strength to get through this and then I would make a plan to escape. I stood with all the grace expected of a Minister's daughter. I let my diplomatic smile take over my face and turned to Heather. "Alright. I'm ready."

∞

Heather guided me from the train and her two giant cronies followed behind us with my suitcase in hand. Heather kept our arms crooked together as we moved through the crowd of people at the station and I didn't know if it were for my protection or to ensure I didn't run.

Whatever fantasies I may have harbored of running away quickly disappeared. There were too many people and I couldn't tell who was a Royal or not. I had always believed that the Capital was for Royals only, but surely there couldn't have been this many of them. I wondered what else my father had failed to include in my education.

I found myself sticking close to Heather. There was a carriage waiting for us outside the station. The horses were impressively tall and well-groomed. The coachman was dressed in a black suit and matching hat. His shoes were polished to perfection. He said nothing as he opened the carriage door for us.

Heather and I sat opposite of the two men. I was beginning to wonder if they were mutes, for they were as silent as the dead. One of them kept a vice-like grip on my leather suitcase.

I folded my hands on my lap and glanced at Heather.

Heather could sense my question. "Now we will go to Madam Desjardins," She said as the carriage pulled away from the station. "I will warn you now that Madam is a Royal, so I expect you to treat her with the utmost respect."

I shivered. "Yes, of course."

I spent the rest of the ride in silence. I grasped my dress nervously, creasing the fabric and releasing it over and over. The curtains were drawn over the windows and I did not care to peek out and see the Capital up close. I sat rigid and obedient, too exhausted to make an attempt at small talk.

The carriage stopped, and the door opened a moment later. The coachman took my hand to help me out and then Heather. We stood in front of a three-story townhome, the rows of housing continuing down the block. The sidewalk was made of uniform paving stones and the small garden was edged with a tall, thin hedge.

I swallowed nervously, looking up at the white brick facade. There were wrought iron bars on the window and the door was painted black to match. The house was unmarked, no signage or symbols to indicate what took place inside.

"Shall we?" Heather asked with a smile, gesturing forward.

I nodded slowly. I couldn't help but glance behind me to see if there was any chance escape, but the two men created a solid wall behind us. My heart trembled and my stomach turned. I forced my eyed ahead of me, trying not to let my fear show as we walked up the steps.

Heather knocked her knuckles against the wooden door, and it opened immediately.

A well-dressed butler stood there with a polite, tight-lipped smile. He bowed his head. "Ms. Igwe, so happy that you have returned."

"Thank you, Roger," Heather said, nodding her head to him.

"And this must be the newest member of the house?" Roger continued, his eyes lighting up when he saw me.

I blushed, but thankfully Heather cut me off before I could speak. "Yes, Miss. Violet will be joining us for a while."

Roger nodded again and locked the door behind us. He went back to the mantel that he must have been polishing before we arrived.

The house was grand, even more so than a Minister's house. The dark wooden trim gleamed, thick plush carpets in the center of every room, the dark wooden floor clean enough to reflect our shadows. The furniture was embroidered with floral patterns. The fireplace was not in use and I could see not a speck of ash. It smelled like a rich perfume and the lemon oil that Roger was using to clean the mantel.

Heather caught my gaze. "Lovely, isn't it?"

I nodded. It was a far cry from the bloody hovel that I had imagined all night. I felt silly for letting my mind get carried away with me. If Madam Desjardins was a Royal, then there would be no doubt she would live with such luxuries.

"Follow me," Heather ordered. She led me down the hall to a spacious washroom.

The ivory and black tiled room was in the same impeccable condition as the sitting room. Heather busied herself by starting a warm bath. I caught a glimpse of myself in the mirror and held in a shriek. My curly hair was knotted and wild, my eyes were circled with black, my lips dry and chapped and a purple thumb-shaped bruise marked the center of my throat.

"Here, a bath will revive you." Heather stood and wiped her hands on a fluffy white towel. "I'll get the kitchen to prepare breakfast for you." The door closed behind her with a click.

I flew to the tiny window, standing on the toilet and pulling with all my might. I scrambled for a moment before realizing it was locked. I fumbled with the latch, but it wouldn't budge. "No, no, no!" I hissed, prying at the metal until my fingers were numb.

Finally, I sank down, defeated. Where was I planning to go, anyway? My shoes were pinching my feet, meant for sitting at dinner parties, not escaping kidnappers. I had no jacket, no identification, and no idea where I was. I rested my forehead against the tiled wall, letting a single frustrated tear fall down my cheek.

I stripped off my wrinkled dress and undergarments. I felt like an animal, not having seen a toilet or a sink in an eternity. I relieved myself before sinking into the warm bath. The water enveloped me, and I let out a sigh. This tub was deeper than the one I had back at the manor; I sunk down all the way until my cheeks touched the water. There was a slight aroma of lavender. A soft sponge and soap sat on the shelf beside me.

I scrubbed my body and hair clean, then continued to soak until the water went cold. The longer I stayed hidden in the bathroom, the longer I would have before needing to speak to Heather again. I argued with myself, knowing that I shouldn't blame her for my capture. It was my father who sent me away and contracted me to the mysterious Madam Desjardins.

There was a knock at the door. "Miss Violet, are you alright?" Heather asked.

"Yes," I called out softly and forced myself to leave the comfort of the water.

"Good, I was worried you might have drowned," Heather said and let out a chuckle.

I frowned, wondering how drowning could possibly be funny. Had other captives drowned themselves in fear of what would come next? I shivered and wrapped a towel around myself.

"Are you decent? May I come in?" Heather asked. "I brought you some fresh clothing."

I glanced at the wrinkled dress I had left carelessly on the floor. "Yes, please come in."

Heather opened the door and pocketed a ring of keys. She must have locked the door when she left. I truly was a prisoner here. Bundled in her arms was a burgundy dress. It was one of my favorite dresses from home. I wondered who my father had instructed to pack a bag for me. Heather handed me the clothes and left without a word.

Once I dressed and dried and pinned up my hair, Heather took me to a small dining room. It was not formal, just a small round table with four chairs. Someone had laid out a hearty breakfast of eggs, sausages, potatoes, cheese and fruit.

The aroma made my stomach cramp and my lips tremble. It was a large portion, and I ate every bite. It took all my willpower to eat slowly and delicately, as a well brought up lady should.

Heather sat across from me, watching me and sipping black tea. When I finally pushed the plate away and sank back into the chair, Heather smiled. "How was that?"

"Delicious," I replied, and I meant it.

"Good," Heather said. "Bloodletters need to have a hearty diet to keep in good health."

I grimaced and stared at the cup of tea in front of me. I pushed my anger towards my father and not Heather.

"If you're all done, I have prepared a room for you upstairs," Heather continued. "Madam will see you when she has a moment, but right now I would suggest getting some sleep."

I had no strength to argue. "Very well."

Heather led me upstairs and down a narrow hall. There were half a dozen identical doors to choose from. She stopped at one and unlocked it. "I know it's not what you're used to," she said apologetically. "But please try to make yourself comfortable."

The room was tiny. About the size of my closet back at the manor. There were two single beds with a dresser beside each. My suitcase was on the left side. There was a blue quilt folded at the end of the bed. The wallpaper had a floral pattern that matched the gauzy curtains. Immediately, I tried to open the window, but it was locked as well.

With a sigh, I settled down on the bed and closed my eyes. I fell asleep instantly.

∞

I woke up hours later. I sat up with a jolt, momentarily forgetting where I was. My heart sank as the events from the past day came back to me. I flung myself back onto the mattress and stared at the ceiling.

I remembered my suitcase, sitting propped up against the footboard. I opened it to find three other dresses and was surprised to see that they were my favorites. Underneath, several pairs of stockings and undergarments, and a sweater folded neatly.

Then, at the very bottom, a piece of paper wrapped in a silk scarf. I choked, fresh tears springing to my eyes. It was the photo of my mother that I kept tucked into my mirror. On the back, there was a message scrawled. *Don't give up, Violet. Mrs. B.* Mrs. Barber had been the one to pack my suitcase. What had father told her? If she was the only one who knew the truth, then her safety would be in jeopardy.

A clatter rang out as something fell from the silk scarf. It looked like a ring; I dropped to my knees to grab it before it rolled under the bed. When I opened my hand, my heart leaped into my throat. It was my mother's amber ring. The one thing that my father had allowed me to keep of her. Mrs. Barber must have taken it from my trinket box. As the daughter of a minister, I had countless precious jewels, but this was the only one that meant anything to me.

I whispered a prayer of gratitude to the old woman and pressed the photo against my chest. I folded the photo back into the scarf and put it at the bottom of the top drawer of the dresser. I piled my undergarments on top of it to make sure it wouldn't be found. I slipped the amber ring on my right hand. It was made of silver filigree with a large amber stone in the center.

Once all my belongings were away, I shoved the suitcase under my bed and sat. How long would it be before Heather came for me? I thought about trying the window again but shrugged the hope away. Maybe Madam Desjardins would be a reasonable woman and agree to let me go. After all, I was a Minister's daughter, not some common girl. But, if she agreed to cancel the contract, where could I go? It wasn't as if I could return to the manor after what my father had done. I chewed my bottom lip nervously.

The turning doorknob snapped me from my worries. I looked up, expecting to see Heather, but instead, it was a slight, pale girl who looked younger than me.

The girl gasped, her round blue eyes growing wider. "Excuse me!" She exclaimed and her white face flushed red. "I didn't realize you were in here. Heather told me I was getting a new roommate." She trailed off.

The other half of the room had been so impeccably tidy that I hadn't even considered that someone might have been using it. I stood and smoothed out my dress. "Not at all," I said, recalling countless etiquette lessons. "It is your room too, after all. My name is Violet," I hesitated, not knowing if I should tell her I was an Ackerman. I decided against it for now.

The girl looked relieved. "Amelia." She shook my hand lightly. "A pleasure." Amelia was very thin, pale, and slightly shorter than me. Her brown hair hung straight, falling past her shoulders. She wore a casual white cotton dress and brown loafers.

A million questions came to mind, but I held them back. I didn't want to seem rude or desperate. The silence stretched between us and I began to worry about what to say next. Judging by her expression, she was just as anxious.

"Well, I hope you don't snore." Amelia laughed nervously.

I forced a weak giggle. "Not to worry, I don't." More unbearable silence. "Ahem, anyway," I continued. "Do you happen to know where Heather would be? She said she would to take me to see the Madam."

Amelia's lips pressed into a thin line. She hesitated and then spoke. "Oh, I see. Well, Heather is busy all the time. I've been here a year and I still can never seem to find her when I need her."

"A year?" I breathed.

Amelia nodded. "You, uh, you do know why you're here, don't you?"

"Yes," I said. I couldn't look her in the eye.

"It's really not so bad when you get used to it," Amelia added.

There was a knock at the door. The knock that I remembered distinctly as Heather's. The door opened and confirmed my guess. "Oh, Amelia!" Heather looked surprised to see my new roommate. "You're back already? Has Dr. Coleman cleared you for tomorrow?"

"Yes, the tests are fine," Amelia replied. "I was just going to rest before dinner."

"Fine, fine." Heather waved her hand and turned her attention to me. "Violet, I'm glad you're awake. Madam Desjardins will see you now."

FOUR

I MET MADAM DESJARDINS IN HER STUDY.

The door was open. It was a small, dark room with burgundy wallpaper. A small stained-glass window and a single lamp illuminated the space with a warm glow. The Madam was sitting at a mahogany writing desk, recording something in a large journal.

"Excuse me, Madam? May I introduce Miss Violet Ackerman," Heather said.

Madam Desjardins looked up from her work. "Ah, yes, please come in."

Heather nudged me over the threshold with a firm hand. "Relax, she won't bite." Heather whispered to me. She stepped back and shut the door.

I was alone with Madam. My eyes adjusted to the dim lighting as I stared straight ahead, not daring to make eye contact.

Madam Desjardins stood. She was much older looking than I imagined. She was delicate, with pale wrinkled skin and snow-white hair styled in a twist with a golden hair comb. Her floor length black gown had a high lace collar and long sleeves. Her lips were painted red and her eyes were dusted in gray. The string of pearls around her neck glinted in the lamplight. She was a picture of elegance and class.

My mouth went dry. "Good afternoon," I forced myself to whisper.

Madam Desjardins smiled. It was a tight-lipped smile that showed more in her eyes that her mouth. She seemed amused as she looked me up and down. "Miss Violet Ackerman, is it?" She said finally. Her voice was stronger than I had expected.

I nodded. "Yes, Madam." I kept my hands behind my back and clenched them tightly.

Madam gestured to a table with two chairs opposite the writing desk. "Please, sit down."

I obeyed dumbly, sitting and settling my trembling hands on my lap. I glanced at her repeatedly as she moved about the small study. There was a tea set on a serving cart. Madam laid out two cups on a silver tray and poured the first cup.

"Would you like some tea?" She asked me.

"Oh, no, thank you," I stammered. Shouldn't she have servants for this?

Madam chuckled under her breath. "Please don't be shy, girl," she said. "I will be feeding you for the next while, after all."

"Oh." My cheeks burned. "Very well, I'll have one. Please." I added hastily.

She brought the tray to the small table and sat down.

I tried not to tap my feet impatiently. I kept my hands calm enough to take the tea from her before quickly hiding them under the table again. I was just served tea by a Royal – a Royal who technically owned me for the next year and a half.

"So, how was your trip?" Madam asked as she poured milk into her tea.

I almost laughed. Her tone was light as if she had asked how I enjoyed a holiday. "Fine," I replied, squeezing my knees. I bit my lip but couldn't control the outburst that came next. "Why is this happening? What did I do wrong? Why would my father sell me like this?" I gasped, clapping a hand to my mouth.

Madam Desjardins didn't seem shocked by my explosion. She finished stirring her tea and setting the silver spoon into the saucer before looking up. "You did nothing wrong, child."

I inhaled and choked. I wanted to ask a million questions, but they were lodged in my throat.

"As for your father, I cannot speak to his motives," the lady continued. "But if he sent you away in the manner he did, maybe it's best for you to be here." Her green eyes flicked up to me.

I shrank back in the mahogany chair. "Yes," I whispered.

"I assure you, Miss Ackerman, you will be safe here." Madam Desjardins said.

My lips trembled, but I would not cry in front of her. I was strong. I was the educated, politically savvy young lady that my mother had raised. I stood up straight and set my shoulders. I put aside the issues with my father and whatever terrible reasons he had betrayed me for. I had to focus on now. I had to focus on the future. "So, you signed a contract to become my guardian?" I asked.

Madam tipped her head slightly. "I guess you could put it that way," she answered. "Though it is more of an employment contract."

"And when I turn nineteen?" I fired out my next question.

"Then, as a legal adult, you can decide whether or not you will continue employment with me." She raised her eyebrows. "This isn't a prison," she added. "You will be paid, and I will hold the amount in trust until you decide to leave."

"What will become of me until then?"

Madam sipped her tea. "Well, you will begin training as a Bloodletter," she said. "Heather will guide you through the process."

"And if I refuse?"

Madam sipped her tea again and set down the china cup carefully. The silence filled the room.

I held my breath. Suddenly, the Royal side of her was visible. I could feel the energy shift around us.

"Well," She said. "If you choose to leave us, you would be homeless, penniless, and lost in a city of strangers."

A shiver ran down my spine.

"Not every Royal is as kind as me, Miss Ackerman," she said. "I realize that you may be ignorant in the ways of the world, but I would not test the waters so quickly."

My stomach felt heavy. I bowed my head and stared at my teacup. "I apologize, Madam." I ran my finger around the golden rim of the cup.

"You're not the first fiery girl to walk into my house," Madam continued. "And I admire your spirit. However, monsters within these walls are nothing compared to the monsters that lurk beyond."

∞

Dinner was served in a formal room with a long table. There were twelve place settings in total, but only five were filled when Heather brought me in. The center of the table was filled with a wide selection of food. Roast lamb, spinach salad, mixed vegetables, hot

42

bean soup, and bread. The three young women and two men had already helped themselves and were making idle conversation when we arrived.

Heather cleared her throat, and they went silent. "Good evening everyone, I would like to introduce the newest member of our family." One girl grimaced at this description. "Miss Violet."

Five pairs of eyes looked at me with uninterested expressions.

I forced a small smile, directly mostly at Amelia, who was sitting further down the table. Thankfully, she smiled back. "Good evening," I said.

Heather patted me on the shoulder. "Go help yourself. I will be along shortly."

I whipped my head around to protest, but Heather had already gone in the direction of the kitchen. I clenched my fists at my side and took a seat across Amelia. She was looking slightly better than she had this afternoon.

The tension in the room was palpable. I let my mask of indifference fall into place as I took a bowl of soup and a piece of bread.

"Stick to the meat." One man said quietly. "You'll be needing the protein."

I glanced at him. "Thank you."

"I didn't say it for you," he shot back. "I just don't want to see Amelia lose another roommate."

I held in a gasp, noticing that Amelia's face turned bright red, and took a slice of lamb.

The room was filled with the sound of clinking forks and knives. I looked up through my eyelashes at each of the attendees in turn. The man who spoke about the meat looked to be older than me, his short hair and beard tinted with a few gray hairs. He had broad shoulders that stretched his jacket to the limit. Beside him was a teenage girl with a gaunt face and watery eyes. She had two sweaters layered over her dress and still shivered. The teenage boy beside her was wearing gloves and fumbling to keep his soup spoon steady. His brown hair was starting to recede. Furthest down the table was a girl with long blond hair. She was the only person at the table with some color to her cheeks, and I suspected it was makeup.

The blond cleared her throat and pushed her empty plate away. "So anyway, as I was saying before we were interrupted." She sent an icy glance in my direction. "I heard from Beatrice. I received her letter this morning. She says she's doing well since retiring. Found a job as a seamstress for a Royal, apparently."

The girl in the sweater nodded and murmured a reply.

Amelia whimpered, her trembling hands trying to butter a slice of bread.

The blond clenched her teeth. "Oh Gods, what's wrong now?" She spat.

Amelia hiccupped and dropped the knife with a clatter.

"Greta, please, watch your temper." The bearded man hissed.

"What, just because Rose croaked, I can't talk about my former roommate?"

Amelia gasped and buried her head in her hands. Her shoulders shook violently.

"Greta!" The other voices joined together.

Greta crossed her arms over her generous bosom. "What?" She said with a sniff. "She needs to get over it. Bloodletters die. It's part of the risk, in case you haven't noticed."

My mouth went dry, and I struggled to chew the lamb.

Amelia made a strangled sound.

"Greta!" a new voice shouted. Heather was standing in the doorway with a platter of tarts and fruit. Her eyes blazed.

Greta didn't shrink back. She stood and threw her napkin onto her plate. "I was just leaving anyway," she said. "You can all enjoy the pity party."

Heather didn't stop her as the blond walked out of the dining room and stomped upstairs.

∞

I laid awake that night, despite my exhaustion.

Amelia arrived shortly after midnight. She was as silent as a ghost as she unpinned her hair, changed into a nightdress and slipped into bed.

I was facing the wall and pretending to be asleep as she settled in for the night. I chewed my lip, wondering if I should say something. The rest of dinner had been a somber affair. Heather tried to revive conversation, but all her attempts failed. I felt guilty being the replacement.

Before I could talk myself out of it, I rolled over to face Amelia. She was sitting up in bed brushing her long hair. "Hey," I whispered softly.

Amelia jumped, her round eyes snapping open. "Oh, I'm sorry, did I wake you?"

I shook my head and sat up. "No. I can't sleep."

Amelia smiled softly. "I couldn't either, my first few nights."

"You've been here for a year, you said, right?" I asked.

She nodded. "A year, two weeks and four days." She laughed bitterly. "Not that I'm counting."

"Why did you come here?" I couldn't help myself.

Amelia hesitated.

"I'm sorry, wasn't my place." I apologized hurriedly.

Amelia shook her head. "No, it's ok. It's just that I remember asking Rose the same thing." Her voice shook but her face remained strong.

I went cold, remembering that this girl named Rose once slept in the bed I was laying in.

Amelia sighed and set her brush down. "I ran away from home last winter," she explained. "My family lived in a town not far from the border of the Capital, in Chwetir. I knew that Blood Houses were always looking for fresh meat. Girls my age especially, according to the rumors I heard at school." She sighed. "So, I snuck onto a train and made my way here. The first few Houses turned me away." She glanced at me. "As you can imagine, it's expensive to feed and house Bloodletters." She shrugged. "But finally, while I was walking the streets, starving and exhausted, Heather ran into me while she was doing errands. She brought me back here, and that's how it started."

I was silent, letting her story sink in.

"Maybe it's not the best fate, but it was better than being at home. My family was very poor, you see, and I had five other sisters. I was the oldest and my father was pressuring me to get married, but we had nothing for a dowry," Amelia rattled on and I felt as if she was happy to get this story off her chest. "When I'm older, I'll take my allowance from Madam and get married." A small smile played around her lips.

I couldn't help but smile. I hugged my legs to my chest. "I hope that works out for you," I said sincerely. I was out of practice when it came to speaking to girls my age. I was well versed in a typical light conversation at fundraising galas and dinner parties but finding a true connection with someone was something I had never been good at. All my life my best friend had been my mother, and now she was gone.

Amelia sniffed and wiped her eyes. "What about you?"

I started. Amelia hadn't grown up in Wythtir and so she had no idea who I was. Who I used to be? I swallowed. To make an attempt at friendship, she deserved the truth. "Well," I said slowly as I tried to form the story. "I'm from Wythtir. My father is a Minister."

Amelia gasped.

"My mother died." I paused and checked the clock. "Twelve days ago." Fresh pain erupted in my heart; the feeling was still raw. "Anyway, my father, he always hated me. He never said it, but I knew he did. And he sent me here."

Amelia let out the breath she had been holding. "Oh, Violet. I'm so sorry."

I shrugged it off. I shoved the feelings away again. The tiny bed creaked as I stretched my legs out in front of me. I played with the cuff on my nightdress. I wondered why everyone else was here. Surely Bloodletting was not an ideal path for any of us, but here we were just the same.

Amelia yawned and settled down into bed. "Well, I would try to get some sleep if I were you," she said. "Heather will run you ragged with training."

I appreciated the warning. "Alright, good night." I turned over and wrapped my quilt around myself.

Amelia laughed and whispered in a singsong. "Goodnight, sleep tight. Don't let the Royals bite."

FIVE

MY TRAINING WITH HEATHER STARTED AT DAWN.

I was shaken from my sleep with a firm hand. I bolted, gasping and nearly crying out before I locked eyes with her. She put a finger to her lips and gestured to Amelia, who was sleeping peacefully. I followed Heather out of the room and down the hall to a communal washroom.

The floor was cold. I shivered in my cotton nightdress.

"For the first week, we will get you accustom to the House and do some testing," Heather told me as she retrieved a bundle of clothes from a closet.

The sight of a plain black skirt, blouse, and apron made me wrinkle my nose in disgust.

49

"There will be none of that, Miss Violet," Heather reprimanded before I could object. "Until you're cleared for Bloodletting, you must earn your keep in other ways."

Once I washed myself and dressed, Heather took me downstairs to the kitchen. There, the cook was busy preparing breakfast for the household. Roger, the butler, was supervising and reading a long grocery list.

The cook looked up from the dough he was kneading. "Good morning, Heather."

"Good morning, Vincent," Heather responded. She handed me a plate filled with food. "Here, eat up. We have lots to do today."

I sat at the wooden table watching Heather and Vincent move about each other in an unrehearsed dance. Roger came and went, always muttering something under his breath. "Is it just the three of you in this big house?" I asked. I didn't dare ask about the huge men who had vanished since I arrived; if I never saw them again, it would be too soon.

Heather looked over her shoulder. "No, there's the coachman, Mr. McCray, he also takes care of the grounds. And the maid Miss Prescott, I'm sure you'll see her around," she explained. Her sleeves were rolled up, and she was elbow deep in dirty dishes. "Everyone around here does double duty."

"Keeps us out of trouble." Vincent laughed. He clapped his hands together and a cloud of flour rained down.

The cook and Heather exchanged a meaningful glance that I pretended to miss. I swallowed the last of my bread. "What am I going to do today?" I asked. My father was elected when I was five, so I had hardly had to lift my finger since. I spent my days studying, riding, and socializing. I had never scrubbed a pot in my life.

"I'll take you with me to the market this morning, then you have an appointment with Dr. Coleman this afternoon," Heather said, drying her hands.

I breathed a tiny sigh of relief. Shopping? I could do that.

∞

Turns out, shopping wasn't as easy as I thought.

Doing the grocery shopping for an entire household in a crowded market, even with the help of Heather and Mr. McCray, took hours.

By the time we returned, my blistered feet were aching in the leather boots that Heather had promised would be much more practical than the shoes I wore on my feet when I was whisked away. She also commented that I should be grateful that it wasn't winter, or else I might not have come with all my toes intact.

I pried off the boots and sank down at the wooden table. The stone floor cooled my aching feet.

Vincent was humming and preparing soup for lunch. My stomach growled in response to the smell of beans, tomatoes, spinach, and spices. "How was shopping?" Vincent asked while keeping his attention of the simmering brew.

"Fine." I groaned.

Vincent laughed; his belly shook. "So, not fine, then?" He snickered. "Oh, dear, I told Heather that a well-bred girl like you wasn't used to work."

I bristled. "I kept up just fine, thank you."

"Well, I'd say that is a generous statement."

I scowled at Heather as she walked in with a bag of flour under each arm. "Hey, I didn't ask to be here, ok? I'm only here because –"

"Because of your father?" Heather cut me off, dropping the flour and dusting off her hands. "No, that's not it is it? Madam told me; you know. You can leave anytime you want, she said. But you won't because you're scared."

I bit my tongue. It was my first instinct to deny it, but she wasn't lying. I sighed and traced a knot in the table with my finger.

"Don't be so hard on her, Heather," Vincent chided. "She'll adjust, just like you did."

Heather looked away, speechless.

Vincent poured a bowl of soup and set it down in front of me gently. "Here you go, dear." He said. "Eat up. Folate, riboflavin, and B vitamins are all essential to keeping your blood healthy. I cook everything with a Bloodletter's needs in mind."

I ate the soup, grateful for the distraction from Heather. She slammed cupboard doors as she put away canned goods, jars of jam, pickles, and other preserves.

I stirred the soup, watching the kidney beans and barley circle around my spoon. Heather was right. I could have marched out of Madam Desjardins' study and right out the front door if I wanted to yesterday. I could have run off when Heather turned her back to barter for eggs only an hour ago, but I didn't. Madam was right. I had nothing to my name and nowhere to go. I needed her, for now.

8

Late in the afternoon, Heather took me a room to meet Dr. Coleman.

"The doctor is a Royal, so I expect you to treat him with the utmost respect," Heather said. It was the first time she had spoken to me since snapping in the kitchen.

I nodded. Once I finished the rest of my chores, I changed out of the plain clothes and into a more presentable dress from my suitcase. I treated my blisters with salve before squeezing them back into my new boots.

The room was white and had a vinegary smell in the air. The radiator hissed and clanked in the corner. The furniture comprised a desk, two chairs, and a cot; white cabinets hung on the walls. Dr. Coleman was sitting in one chair. His thinning hair was salt and pepper gray. He was thin and dressed in white. He looked like one would expect a doctor to look, except for the intensity hiding behind his eyes.

"Good afternoon, Miss Violet," Dr. Coleman said. His voice was gravelly and low.

Heather left without a word.

I was both grateful to be free of her and terrified of being handed off to the doctor.

"Don't be afraid, child," the doctor said. He pulled a pair of round wire-framed glasses from the pocket of his lab coat and cleaned them with a handkerchief. "Just a few pricks today, nothing to worry your pretty head over."

I nodded, fidgeting in my boots.

The doctor gestured to the chair. "Take a seat, and we'll start."

The first half of my appointment was fairly routine. He asked about my health, my family, took standard measurements and all the other ordinary things one would expect at a yearly physical. One perk of being in a Minister's family was having funded medical care. Mother had always reminded my brothers and me of this blessing every time one of us fell ill and received prompt treatment for ailments that other children perished from.

Dr. Coleman scribbled some notes down on his clipboard. When I responded he listened intently, tapping the board on his knee and making appropriate comments or sounds when I paused.

When I was sure I couldn't give him any more information, he capped his pen. "Well, Miss Violet," he said. "It sounds like you are in very good health and would make a great candidate to be a Bloodletter," he explained. "Madam Desjardins rarely signs a contract sight unseen; however, based on your upbringing and medical history, I would agree that she made a fine choice."

I managed a weak smile. I was sure he meant this as a compliment, but I felt like a prized pig being prepped for the slaughter.

The doctor stood. "Please lay down and expose both arms to me."

I flushed. Dr. Coleman got right to business.

"Please don't be bashful," he added. "I'm a doctor. A professional, I assure you."

With some difficulty, I rolled up my sleeves and laid down on the cot. The pillow felt as if it were stuffed with newspapers and the sheet had the same vinegary smell as the air. I watched the doctor open and close cabinets, filling a tray with instruments that I could only imagine would be as painful as they looked. I closed my eyes, trying to ignore the clicking of metal and rustling of paper.

"Try to relax, Miss Violet," Dr. Coleman said.

I opened my eyes and felt my mouth go dry.

In the metal tray were needles, a syringe, rubber tubing, glass vials, and gloves. Dr. Coleman pulled on the gloves with a snap and pushed up his glasses with the palm of his hand. "Have you ever had a blood sample taken before?"

I dumbly shook my head no.

The doctor chuckled. "No, I expected not. Most affluent families are exempt from random sampling." He sorted through his tools and I tried not to faint.

My body was trembling. It was taking all the willpower I possessed not to run screaming from the white room. I gnawed on my lip. "Will it hurt?" I croaked.

Dr. Coleman shook his head. "Not any more than a fly bite, if I do it correctly."

I made a noise in my throat but couldn't form words.

"Please relax, young lady," Dr. Coleman instructed. "It will be over soon." He attached the syringe and the tubing together and slipped it into a hole in the vial's lid. It was the oddest contraption that I had ever seen.

Dr. Coleman held my wrist with one hand and aimed the long needle towards my arm.

I saw stars and fainted.

It felt like only a blink when my eyes fluttered open a few minutes later. There was a cold cloth pressed to my forehead and my inner arm was wrapped in bandages. Dr. Coleman was sitting at the desk with his back to me. There were four of the vials on the desk, the fifth was in his hand.

I squeaked. My stomach turned at the sight of the dark red fluid. My blood.

The doctor turned with surprise. "Oh good, you're awake. I was wondering when you'd come to. How are you feeling?"

"Fine, just a bit dizzy," I replied and tried to sit up.

Dr. Coleman rushed to my side. "Ah, ah, ah!" he tutted. "We will have none of that. You just gave me a significant amount of blood. You need to rest."

I grimaced and glanced at the vial in his hand. "How much?"

"Oh, not enough to cause any damage," he replied. "But you will feel woozy for the next few hours, so please lay down."

I followed his instructions and stared at the ceiling. The academic in me was bursting with questions and the silence was unbearable. "What will you do with it now?"

Dr. Coleman looked up from his notes. "I will send it for testing. We should have the results back in a week or so."

"Testing? Like a taste test?" I asked.

Dr. Coleman let out a hearty chuckle. "Oh, my Gods, no!" he said. "No, they go for testing to ensure that your blood is safe for consumption. There are strict policies in place for these things, you know. Since introducing the Bloodletting Regulation Act, but I guess that was before your time." He paused. "Over a hundred years now, actually."

The same laws that Heather mentioned. The same laws I had been ignorant to throughout all my training. "Why?"

Dr. Coleman looked surprised. "The regulations ensure the safety of the Royals who drink your blood. After all, many diseases can be transmitted that way and we need to make sure they don't spread," he explained. "It was before your time, obviously, but when I was younger, I remember that Blood Houses were founded by just about anyone and the Royals were getting sick from contaminated blood. The blood taxes were abolished shortly after that. These laws protect the Royals and they also protect people like you." He raised his thick eyebrows at me. "Now Bloodletters have rights, a reasonable pay, and safety. Not like it was before." He trailed off.

"I see," I said and then stammered. "Wait, you remember what it was like before? How is that possible?"

Dr. Coleman laughed again. "I believe the legend goes that the Gods blessed us with longevity, beauty, and strength. Am I right?"

I closed my eyes and pressed my hand against my chest. My heart was pounding. "How old are you?"

"One hundred and sixty-eight," Dr. Coleman answered. "But I should tell you it's incredibly rude to ask a Royal their age."

My stomach twisted. The great number was nearly incomprehensible.

The doctor sighed. "Well, enough of a history lesson for today, Miss," he said. "That isn't my place, anyway." He packed up the vials in a bag.

I sat up, but my vision blurred, and I was forced to lay back down. The room was spinning around me. "What now?"

"We will find out in a week's time. For now, stay here and rest. I will call for Heather to collect you."

SIX

HEATHER DID NOT WAIT FOR THE TEST RESULTS TO COME BACK BEFORE STARTING MY TRAINING.

Each morning started the same. She would wake me up before the sun rose and we would clean, cook and prepare the house for the day ahead. She worked wordlessly. The easy conversation she made with me the first day had vanished.

"For now, I'm your boss," she had told me. "Now that you are in training, we cannot be friends."

I respected her method and followed her orders to the best of my abilities. I scrubbed pots, washed laundry, mended clothing and dusted the rooms until my hands were raw. I dared not complain to her about my dry cracking skin, knowing it would only earn me a snide remark about my luxurious childhood.

I lunched with the rest of the residents of the house who seemed to attend in an unpredictable cycle. I was always left out of the conversation.

I dedicated my afternoons to training.

The first day we met in the library. It was a cozy room filled with shelves that bowed under the weight of countless books. She dropped an armful of books in front of me.

"Read these, let me know when you're done."

I guessed that she didn't think I was a fast reader or take into account that all of my life I had been studying history and politics. I breezed through the content, many of the books were identical to the volumes I had read in the manor.

It was all the same stuff. The war, the forming of Inwaed, the Royals, and us, the commoners. I stifled a yawn while wondering how this stale information that could be found in any classroom across the country would prepare me for Bloodletting.

It was past dinnertime when Heather returned. "You read it all?" She asked.

I nodded.

"Good, now forget it."

Heather let me stew over her obscure command the rest of the night.

The second day we met in the library again.

"So," Heather began. "Did you do what I said?"

I crossed my arms. "You can't expect me to forget years of lessons overnight," I argued. "What would be the purpose in that? Everyone knows the history of Inwaed. Everyone knows about the Royals."

"Do they?" Heather hissed. She planted her hands on the mahogany table and stared me in the eye. "Do they really?" She pushed off the table and paced around before continuing. "I believe it was only a few days ago that you didn't even know what a Bloodletter was."

I flushed. I hated admitting to ignorance.

"In fact, you also seemed to think the Capital was some magical place meant only for the Royals," she chuckled. "If that were the case, where would the blood come from?"

I was silent.

Heather whirled on me, slamming her fist on the table with so much force that I jumped. "Where does the blood come from, Violet?" She shrieked.

"I didn't know!" I gasped.

"Didn't know? Or didn't care?" Heather hissed.

My hands were trembling now. I wanted to hide my burning face from her icy glare. I had known that Royals had to drink our blood to survive, but I had never wondered where the blood came from. Who it came from?

"Typical," Heather snorted. "You know, when I saw you, I thought you'd be a fighter. A minister's daughter, stolen away from her home, sold by her own father and thrust into the arms of monsters." She tapped her fingers against the table and sat down to face me. "You're just like everyone else, you know that? Scared."

I bit my tongue.

"What were you going to do if you got your father's title one day?" She asked, her voice barely a whisper. "Were you going to be a noble leader? Work with the Royals for the betterment of the people of your province?" She threw back her head and laughed.

I slouched down to avoid her glare. I had thought like that once. My mother had always told me to become a good leader to win my father's affections. I studied night and day, perfect my public speaking, attended every gala, and did everything I possibly could to be the ideal heir. And it was all for nothing. My pride got the better of me and I retorted. "I knew enough. I would have been great."

Heather's laugher cut off, and she narrowed her eyes at me. "No, don't you dare tell me you knew anything about how this world really works. The Royals only tell you what they want you to know and believe me, you know nothing!"

∞

I skipped dinner and went straight to bed. I couldn't bear to see or speak to anyone. I sat curled up under the quilt and stared at the photograph of my mother. I ran my finger over the edge carefully.

Had she known about Bloodletting? What else had she known about and never shared with me? I was frustrated with my family, but I was frustrated with myself more. Of course, the Royals hid information from their citizens – I couldn't recall a single government in history that hadn't. But as a Minister's daughter, I should have been privy to these secrets, or at least I thought.

I hid the photograph and glanced at Amelia's empty bed. She had known about the Bloodletters. She had run away because of it. She had come willingly into Madam Desjardin's house, prepared to share her blood with the Royals in exchange for money.

I grimaced. How many other girls our age had done the same? How many of them had died from the complications of it?

The door opened. I quickly shut my eyes and pretended to be asleep.

"Hey, Violet." Amelia whispered and nudged my foot gently.

I sighed and opened my eyes. "Yes?"

"I missed you at dinner," she said. "I snuck you something." The pale girl handed me a dinner roll wrapped in a cloth napkin.

My stomach growled. I took the bread from her. "Thanks," I whispered.

"Tough day with Heather?" Amelia asked. She sat on her bed.

I nodded while I chewed.

Amelia smiled. "Don't worry, she's always tough in the beginning."

"What's her problem, anyway?" I asked.

Amelia shrugged. "Oh, I don't know," she replied. "Maybe it's just because she's been doing this longer than we've been alive. Twenty years she's been Bloodletting. I guess it gets to her."

I nearly choked. "Twenty years? She must have quite the account saved up by now. Why doesn't she leave?"

Amelia shrugged again. "Don't know."

I brushed the crumbs off my hands. Now my curiosity had been sparked. "Why would anyone choose to do this?"

Amelia looked away.

"Oh, sorry. I meant why would someone do it for so long?" I corrected myself. "I mean, it's not like this is a sustainable life choice, right?"

"No, it's not. But some people genuinely like Bloodletting." Amelia said after a moment. She caught my look. "Not me but others do. Like Greta."

For some reason I was not surprised by this gossip. "Why would anyone enjoy giving their blood away?"

"I think I know, but it's hard to describe." Amelia drummed her fingers on her knees. She was thinking hard about something, considering what to say next. "If you want, I can show you."

I leaned away discretely. "What do you mean, show me?"

Amelia grinned mischievously.

Without a word, we slipped on shoes, turned off the lamp, and left the room. She led me up to the third floor, taking the stairs carefully and listening for anyone who might catch us.

"We do the Bloodletting on the third floor," Amelia whispered to me. "Madam oversees it and we get checkups from Dr. Coleman every few days. We're quite busy here."

"How many Royals would constitute busy?" I asked.

"Well, that depends. We have our regulars and then others who come and go. They all come at different times. Some prefer days and others come at night. Most of our regulars have a favorite Bloodletter," Amelia explained.

"How many regulars do you have?" I dared to ask.

"About eight. I had to cut down after getting sick," Amelia answered and caught my terrified look. She smiled and rolled her eyes. "It's not like they all come every day. Most Royals only need to have blood once or twice a week."

I nodded. I was getting more knowledge creeping up the stairs with Amelia than I had in two days with Heather in the library.

Amelia stopped at the first door in the hall and listened. When she was sure that it was unoccupied, she let us in. We kept the light off. She led me through the dark room to a door on the side.

"All the Bloodletting rooms are connected with pocket doors," she whispered. "Sometimes several Royals like to come together and make it a social event."

I felt faint.

"Don't worry about that yet." Amelia said and patted my shoulder. "Technically, you need to get cleared by Dr. Coleman before you can give a drop."

I didn't find that comforting, knowing based on the conversation I had with the doctor two days ago that I was likely to be a top candidate.

I heard voices drifting from the other side of the door.

Amelia peeked into the keyhole and gasped. She watched for a moment before pulling away. "Greta is in there with one of her regulars. If you wanted answers to your questions, this should do it for you."

I nodded and pressed my face to the door, squinting to see through the tiny hole.

Greta was lounging on a couch, talking to a man outside the limited area I could see. She was smiling and laughing flirtatiously. I could see a black cuff wrapped tightly around her arm and a familiar length of tubing leading from it.

"I missed you last week, Mr. Quincey," Greta purred. She twirled a length of her hair around her finger.

"And I missed you, my dearest," a man's voice responded. "Your blood truly is the sweetest in the Capital."

Greta turned her face shyly, but I could tell she reveled in the compliment. "You know even though you missed last week, you can't get a double ration today?"

"I know." The man sounded disappointed. "It was my business that kept me away, my dove."

Greta plucked a tiny glass from the table beside her. It resembled a champagne flute, but half the size. She adjusted her cuffed arm and fidgeted.

I clenched my teeth and squinted. It was hard to see what she was doing through the tiny keyhole.

The man who had spoken came into view then. A Royal, dressed in a fine suit on his knees beside the couch. His mouth was half open, lips trembling in anticipation.

Greta handed the tiny glass to him. It was filled to the top with dark red blood. The Royal took it graciously and drank deeply. Greta's eyes widened and her mouth twisted into a smile. Her cheeks flushed.

"Oh, you are the sweetest," the man said after he was done. "There is none other like you."

Greta reached out and brushed his cheek. It took only a flutter of her eyelashes before they were kissing passionately.

I gasped and fell back from the door. My heart was pounding. I couldn't believe what I had witnessed.

"What happened?" Amelia whispered and took a peek for herself. She gasped and looked away. She stood up and hurried me out of the room. "Let's go before someone sees us."

SEVEN

<small>A WEEK LATER DR. COLEMAN SENT MY RESULTS TO MADAM, AND HE CLEARED ME FOR BLOODLETTING.</small>

The news came just as another terrible training session with Heather was set to begin. I was sitting in the library, going over the history of the current Royal family. Every now and then the ruling family would get overthrown or assassinated. The Saxons were the family in power now, ruling for just over one hundred and fifty years.

Our current King was named Luther; he and his queen had ruled for the past four decades, taking the throne after Luther's grandfather had died. His father had never sat on the throne, dying of diseased blood well before his time. It was his death that inspired the

Bloodletting Regulation Act and sweeping reforms to how blood was collected and stored.

This chapter filled in many of the holes from my previous education. In fact, all I had done this week was read and be mercilessly quizzed by Heather on every single fact.

Madam Desjardins accompanied Heather this afternoon.

I bolted up, sitting as still as a statue as Madam sat across from me. Heather lingered behind her.

"Hello, Miss Violet," Madam said. She had an open envelope in her hand. Her long nails were painted a dusty rose pink. "How has your stay been so far?"

"I'm adjusting," I replied after a brief pause to decide how to put my whirlwind of emotions and experiences into words. Every word I tried was so inadequate.

Madam Desjardins nodded. "That is wonderful to hear." She pulled a letter from the envelope. "Well, I have wonderful news for you. Your blood has been accepted and you are now officially a Bloodletter. I'm sure this will spice up for training." She added. "Heather has been doing her best to keep you busy, but I understand that your upbringing has been an excellent prerequisite for her lessons."

I nodded. My face was still but inside I was screaming. My hands were trembling under the table so violently that I was afraid Madam would notice.

While I knew that they would accept my blood, I had harbored the hope that they would reject me.

Since watching Greta give her blood to that Royal man, I could not sleep without being interrupted by nightmares. My stomach turned every time I thought of it.

"I will send out invitations for a Sampling," Madam said. "You will have your debut this Friday, providing I get a quick response. Until then, rest and eat well. Heather will fill you in."

I nodded again, unable to look her in the eye.

Once Madam left us, Heather sat down. "You ready?"

I took a deep breath before bursting into tears.

∞

"It's really not so bad, you know," Amelia said.

I hadn't gone to dinner again.

"And you need to stop skipping meals," she added and handed me a bowl. "I can only sneak out so much."

"I didn't ask you to," I mumbled.

"If you don't eat, you'll die."

I glanced up at her. She was paler than yesterday, and she had dark circles under her eyes. Her expression was grim.

"That's what happened to Rose," she whispered. "She couldn't take giving blood anymore, but she didn't know where else to go. She got sad and stopped eating. Then one morning she didn't wake up." Amelia's voice was thick with emotion, but she didn't let a tear escape her. "Giving as much blood as we do leads to a lot of health problems." She sniffed.

"I'm sorry. I didn't mean to upset you," I said. I took the bowl from the edge of my bed. It was full of beef stew and biscuits. It had gone cold, and the gravy had coagulated, but I ate it all.

Amelia looked satisfied. She smiled at me. "So, they cleared you today, huh?"

I nodded. "How did you know?"

"I may have only been here for a year, but I know that look. It's the same one I had when they told me I was ready to start," she said. "I came here willingly, but it's not like I wasn't nervous or anything."

"What's a Sampling?" I blurted out.

Amelia flushed and then the color drained from her face. "Oh, that," she laughed nervously. "Don't worry about that. It's no big deal." She yawned. "Well, I should get to sleep. I have early appointments tomorrow."

I knew her yawn was fake, but I didn't press for answers. I'd find out soon enough.

∞

"A Sampling is your big debut. All the high-end Blood Houses host them."

Heather dusted my face with powder and blush. My red curls had been elegantly shaped and pulled into a twist. Not a strand was out of place. My long black gown left my neck and arms exposed; the bias cut clung to my body like a second skin. I stared at myself

73

in the mirror. I looked older than seventeen. A small smile played upon my lips when I realized I was the spitting image of my mother.

Heather double checked every little detail; lining my eyes with black and my lips with a rich red. "Ok," she breathed and took a step back. "You're ready."

I glanced at the mirror again. I looked ready on the outside, but on the inside I felt terrified.

According to Heather, twenty royals had accepted the invitation to my Sampling. Madam Desjardin's Blood House was one of the most prestigious in the Capital. The House was known for providing high quality blood in a comfortable setting and none of the Royals minded paying the exorbitant fee. Going to a Blood House was more economical than keeping a personal Bloodletter. The costs of housing and feeding one on top of the Royal's usual staff ran higher than one might expect. Only the wealthiest Royals could afford their own Bloodletter.

"When they call you to enter, you need to be a vision of poise and grace," Heather said as she plucked a stray hair off my dress. "The Royals who are attending tonight paid a premium, and they expect nothing but the best."

"Twenty of them," I whispered.

Heather smiled. "Yes, that is quite the turn out. I expect that Madam hinted at your privileged background to get such a crowd."

"Are they all going to," I grimaced. My words lodged in my throat.

"Drink your blood?" Heather finished for me. "Yes, of course. But this is a Sampling. Don't worry they will not take enough to put your health in danger."

I clenched my hands to stop them from shaking.

"I remember my Sampling," Heather said with a faraway look in her eyes. She smiled. "Now that was a turnout. Madam Desjardins is an excellent businesswoman." She added. "Twenty years later, I still have regulars I met that night." Her voice was dreamy, like the night of her Sampling contained fond memories.

The clock chimed.

"Nine o'clock!" Heather gasped. "Let's get you downstairs. They will begin any minute."

On the ground floor of the house there was a small ballroom that would hold a party of about fifty. The marble floor was polished to perfection. The walls were covered in mirrors in gilded frames that gave the illusion of the room being much larger.

A string quartet was playing in the furthest corner. The guests were dressed in evening finery. The light from the chandelier glinted off gold and diamond jewelry. The men were dressed in black while the women's gowns were shades of red, green or purple, and made of velvet or silk taffeta.

Madam Desjardins cleared her throat, and the music quieted. The guests turned to face her.

I waited outside the double doors, glancing in.

Heather tapped my shoulder and frowned. "Poise and grace," she hissed.

I stood straight and tried not to glare at her. I had attended countless balls in my life, but this was different. All the etiquette training in the world couldn't prepare me for tonight.

"Be yourself, Miss Violet," Heather added. "They know you come from a wealthy background, and they are no doubt expecting you to be a perfect lady. This in your chance to get some clients." She explained. "The more clients you have, the more money you make."

I nodded.

Heather had dressed in a long red gown with lace sleeves. Tiny rosettes traced the high neckline. Her unruly hair had been fastened into a bun. Her lipstick matched her dress. She was breathtaking.

"You look beautiful, Heather," I whispered.

Heather looked surprised. "This is your night, Violet. I'm just here for moral support."

I could tell she wasn't used to compliments. I had been praised my whole life, but they were almost empty words from my father's business partners or potential suitors. I bowed my head and lowered my lashes as my mother had taught me.

My eyes stung. I hadn't had the time to dwell on my mother's death since coming here.

Heather noticed my eyes going misty. "Don't you dare cry! I worked hard on that makeup," she whispered. The woman leaned back towards the door, listening for my introduction.

Madam Desjardins was going on and on, thanking the guests and telling them about me. So far, I hadn't heard her reveal my family name or where I had come from. She was only reassuring them that my blood was the best of the best.

A polite applause rounded off her introduction.

I set my shoulders and held my head high. I slipped my arm through Heather's as she had instructed me. Heather was the mentor of the Blood House, so she could take some credit for well preforming Bloodletters.

I plastered a smile on my face as we entered the ballroom.

The twenty Royals looked me up and down; some did it discreetly, others eyed me down like hungry wolves.

I followed the instructions that Heather was murmuring in my ear. Giving me names and titles much too quickly for me to comprehend.

The music resumed and some Royals went back to their conversations.

Madam Desjardins joined us. The large opal broach at her neck glimmered in the light. "Good evening, ladies."

Heather bowed her head to Madam, and I followed suit.

A middle-aged man dressed in a black suit approached Madam and kissed her gloved hand. "Ah, Madam, it has been ages, hasn't it?"

Madam nodded. "Far too long," she replied and introduced me to the man. "This is Lord Ramsey."

The Baron kissed my hand. "Charmed."

"The pleasure is mine," I managed the correct reply. I hoped he wouldn't notice me shaking. He was very handsome, thought he looked to be as old as my father, I now knew that a Royal's true age was not easily guessed.

"She is quite lovely," he said to Madam as if complimenting her on a well-bred horse.

Madam Desjardins smiled. "Thank you. I was surprised to get your response."

The Baron laughed. "Oh, just because I have the luxury of keeping my own Bloodletter now wouldn't mean I would give up the chance to meet your latest addition." He shot me an appraising look.

I blushed and bowed my head.

The next hour passed slowly. I was introduced to and assessed by every Royal there. I made polite small talk and laughed when appropriate. I felt as if I were walking on glass, but Heather guided me through every step.

I had never been more nervous in my life. When would I be forced to give blood? Would it be some terrible frenzy, or would they patiently wait their turns like the poor at a soup bank?

The housemaid, Miss Prescott carried glasses of champagne on a tray. Heather swatted my hand away when I reached for one and glared at me.

Madam Desjardin rejoined us shortly after that. "I believe it is time," she said to Heather.

Heather nodded and led me out of the ballroom.

Dr. Coleman was waiting for us in the hallway. "Evening, ladies," he said. "How are you feeling, Violet?"

"Fine," I lied. My feet were sore, my hands were sweating, and my jaw was stiff from smiling.

"Excellent!" Dr. Coleman took us to a small antechamber off to the side of the ballroom. His Bloodletting tools lay on a crisp white towel. "Now because this is your first time, we will draw the blood privately. With time, you will become skilled in doing it on your own."

I nodded and sat down. My vision was blurring again.

Heather snapped her fingers in front of my face. "No fainting this time," she added.

I bolted upright again and resisted the urge to rub my eyes.

Heather dabbed the sweat from my face with a towel. "You'll do fine," she added in a softer voice.

I stared at the ceiling as the doctor sat beside me and tied a band tightly around my arm. He pressed my inner arm, looking for veins. I bit my lip, hearing him sort through the needles and humming to himself. I winced, feeling the needle puncture my skin. I squeezed my eyes shut.

Heather patted my hand. "Relax, it will be easier that way."

My heart was pounding. I breathed in and out slowly until the doctor finished. I opened my eyes and gasped at the sight of my blood in a glass jar. I looked down at my arm; he had covered the small wound with a bandage.

Heather wrapped a black satin ribbon over the bandage and tied it with a decorative knot.

I realized I had been holding my breath. I exhaled and leaned back in the chair. The ceiling was swirling above me.

While I rested, Heather, and the doctor poured the blood into tiny crystal cups. They divided the blood evenly amongst twenty-one glasses, each holding what I guessed would be barely a mouthful. "Are you sure you didn't take too much?" I croaked.

Dr. Coleman laughed. "The human body is a strangely resilient machine, Miss Violet."

Heather gave me some water and patted my face dry again. "Alright, the Royals are waiting."

I looped my arm through Heathers and tried not to lean on her too much. My legs felt like rubber and my vision filled with stars.

"Pull it together," Heather whispered.

The maid followed behind us with the tray. The tiny cups were arranged in a spiral.

The music in the ballroom faded as we entered. The twenty Royals turned as one at the sound of the door opening.

Madam Desjardins came to us first. "How are you feeling?" She whispered.

I only managed a tiny nod.

"Ah, excellent, we were hoping you hadn't gotten cold feet."

I recognized the Baron's voice before it was lost in the sycophantic laughter.

Madam Desjardin's jaw clenched a fraction before she stepped back from Heather and me. "Now, it is the moment you've all been waiting for. Miss Violet has some of the purest blood that I have ever presented at my House and I am pleased to be sharing it all with you tonight."

They applauded again. I could feel the anticipation growing.

The maid, Miss Prescott, went around the room with the tray. One by one the crystal cups were selected by Royals, who then went about examining the color and smell.

I felt nauseous and held onto Heather for strength.

The last cup was for Madam Desjardins. She caught my eye briefly before examining the blood.

At some unspoken cue, the Royals began tasting. Some knocked back the entire mouthful while others took dainty sips. There was a low murmur that grew in volume as groups of guests discussed, sipped and talked more.

"A wonderful rich color."

"Such a velvety texture."

"It is a joy to taste such blood."

"Absolutely satisfying."

I heard snippets of the multiple conversations swirling around me. I stared at the floor to avoid their glances. There was a shift in energy, the hairs prickled on the back of my neck.

Feeling the sudden urge to look up, I saw that Madam Desjardins was watching me and gripping the empty cup. There was a flush of color in her pale wrinkled cheeks. Her eyes flickered with the same spark of the other Royals; an unsettling glimpse of the beast that lurked beneath.

EIGHT

After the Sampling, Madam started scheduling appointments for the following week.

Now that I was officially a registered Bloodletter, I no longer had to run errands with Heather. I woke up closer to noon than dawn and was instructed to do nothing but rest for the first few days. Dr. Coleman had explained that it took much longer than a week for a body to fully recover from giving that much blood, and I had done to everything in more power to help it recoup.

Heather's sternness had eased off slightly since the Sampling. The first day she taught me how to care for the puncture wound, what signs of infection looked like, and how to prevent bruising.

"There's nothing more unappetizing to a Royal than seeing the bruise left behind by the last appointment." She told me.

On the third day, my curiosity took hold of me. "Why do Royals need blood?"

Heather faltered, dropping the diagram of arm veins she had been holding. "Excuse me?"

"Why do Royals need to drink blood?" I repeated. I felt like a child again. A girl asking forbidden questions about the Royals after my father's ceremony.

Heather's jaw tightened. "Some things are just better left unknown," she whispered.

I frowned. "That's what my mother said, too."

"Then your mother was a wise woman, Violet," Heather said. "Please, don't question it. Things have always been the way, and they will always stay this way. We give the Royals blood, and in exchange they give us a fair government, protection from invaders, good food and medical care. Without them, we would be lost to chaos once more."

I let Heather's words sink in and they satisfied me for the time being. One day I would know all their secrets, but for now, I would keep silent.

Seven days after my Sampling, my first appointment was booked and several more in the two weeks that followed. Heather and Madam seemed ecstatic with the influx of orders. For me, it was overwhelming.

Friday night, Heather helped me prepare. I dressed beautifully and done my hair and makeup. As I sat in front of the mirror, I couldn't help but feel like a stage actress.

"You look wonderful," Heather said. "Now, for the hard part."

I flinched, remembering my previous lessons. Bloodletting technology had improved a thousand-fold since it began, but the process was still unsettling.

Heather handed me a black silk back that I knew contained a hollow needle and tube. I would have to pierce myself and let the blood flow into the tiny glass that the Royal would drink from. I knew that I must never allow the Royal to feed from me directly, as that was a factor in spreading disease.

I clutched the bag. "I'll be fine," I breathed, more to reassure myself than Heather.

Heather nodded. "You will," she agreed. "But, just in case you need my help, there will be a bell on the side table. I will be just outside in the hall, so please don't hesitate."

I nodded, trying not to think of all the hundreds of things that could go wrong. I had practised inserting the needle a few times, and I was getting better at it. But doing it in front of a hungry audience was something different entirely.

I checked the clock on the wall. It was nearly seven o'clock. "So, who is my client?" I asked.

Heather raised a dark eyebrow. "Why does it matter?" She asked. "Either way, you have to do it."

I shrugged. "I know, I just thought maybe you'd know."

Heather sighed. "The House's records are classified," she explained. "Really, the only people who should know who your clients are, are you and Madam. That prevents jealousy, competition and keeps the matters of the Royals private."

I blinked. "Why would the Royals care who knows? It's not like it's a secret who needs blood."

Heather frowned; I knew she hated talking about the Royals. "Well," She said hesitantly. "For example, I had a client once, many years ago, and his wife hated that he would see a female Bloodletter. She thought he was being unfaithful. Of course, we did nothing but exchange blood, but not all Bloodletters have the same ethics. Madam forbids it, of course."

I felt a tinge of red creeping up on my cheeks. I wondered if Madam knew about Greta's personal relationships with that man I had seen.

"Others don't want their peers knowing that they can't afford to keep their own Bloodletter," Heather added.

The clock chimed and our conversation fell silent.

Heather took me to the third floor. "Your client is waiting in room three." She pointed down the hall. "I'll be sitting here if you need me." She gestured to a chair at the mouth of the hall. "Just ring if you need anything."

I took in a shaky breath.

"You'll do fine," Heather assured me.

I nodded. My success or failure would reflect on her and Madam just as much as it would on me. I walked down to the end of the hall, glancing once over my shoulder. I stopped at the door and set my shoulders. I stood straight, keeping my head held high and closed my eyes. I breathed in and out slowly until I calmed my nerves.

I opened the door without a knock, as Heather told me to do.

The room was small, built for its purpose of hosting only two people. There was a chesterfield against the far wall. The wallpaper, upholstery and carpet were all rich shades of blue. A beautiful golden chandelier illuminated the room.

"Lovely, isn't it?" A voice from the corner startled me.

A man was standing there with his back to me pouring whiskey. Ice cubes clinked against the crystal. He turned and took a sip of the drink. It was the Baron.

"Lord Ramsey." I gasped, nearly taking a step back before remembering myself. I bowed my head. "Forgive me, I wasn't expecting you."

"I thought as much," The Baron chuckled and took another sip. He walked towards me slowly, not hiding the back that he was looking me up and down, inspecting every inch of me.

"How are you doing this evening, my Lord?" I asked. Heather's tips came to my mind in a whirlwind: always make the meeting about them, be attentive, be polite, and flirt but do not mislead.

"Spectacular, my dear," Lord Ramsey replied. He took a step back, his eyes not leaving mine as he sat on the chesterfield. He patted the tufted seat beside him. "Come, let's get to know each other."

I suddenly wished that my first client had been a woman. I smiled and sat a polite distance away from the Baron. I discretely glanced at the small bell that sat on the table to my left. I hoped I would not need to use it.

The Baron twisted a lock of my hair around his finger. "You're beautiful, did you know?"

I cringed inwardly, feigning modesty as I turned my head. "You're too kind, sir," I said. "How have you been since I saw you last?"

Lord Ramsey perked; he was keen to talk about himself, as I soon found out. "Oh, the usual, my dear. Business, politics, all of those boring things."

"Oh, do tell." I hoped that he would reveal more of the Royal's secrets, but he went on about his business partner using company money for gambling. I made responsive noises whenever he paused, letting him direct the conversation in whichever direction he chose.

Over half an hour later, he checked his pocket watch. "Oh my, look at the time. Here I am going on about business. I have bored you stiff."

"Not at all," I replied with a smile.

The Baron inched closer to me on the couch. "Well, I have a wife at home to complain to. I won't torture you anymore." He chuckled. He touched my hair and set his hand on my shoulder. "Is it true I'm your first client?"

I nodded.

Lord Ramsey gulped. "That is perfect," His voice was low and husky.

I leaned back to increase the space between us. The Baron was making me more uncomfortable than any other man ever had. Even Councilor Wentworth's son's drunken advances were more welcome than this. I put a hand on his shoulder gingerly. "Which arm do you prefer, sir?"

The Baron's attention finally snapped away from my chest. "Hm?"

"Which arm, sir?"

Lord Ramsey cleared his throat and sat up straight. He adjusted the collar on his shirt and smooth back his dark hair. "Left, if you please."

I pulled the black bag from a pocket at my hip. My fingers fumbled with the satin drawstring. I ignored the Baron's breathing in my ear. Inside the bag was a black band, fresh bandages, tubing, and a hollow needle. I closed my eyes and sighed.

"Whatever is the matter?"

"I forgot the cup," I answered through gritted teeth.

The Baron laughed. "No matter!" He finished the whisky with a gulp and offered it to me.

This glass was much larger than the tiny crystal cup that blood was to be served in. I wondered how I would measure the amount properly. I bit my lip, but there was no way I would call Heather over something so minor. She'd never let me live it down.

I smiled. "Thank you, my Lord."

I followed the steps that Heather and I had gone over a million times. I pulled the black band tight around my upper arm. I was thankful that the Baron preferred the left arm, because I was still terrible at drawing blood with my other hand. I clenched my teeth and jabbed the vein, showing brightly under my pale skin.

Lord Ramsey sucked in a breath beside me.

I didn't focus on him. I kept my hands steady as I let out the blood into the glass. I counted slowly in my head, a trick that Heather had taught me to ensure I didn't give out too much.

The Baron took the glass from me and I quickly withdrew the needle and applied pressure onto the tiny wound. My heart was pounding in my ears. Stars swirled in my vision. I felt as if I had gulped a glass of wine, there was no other way I could describe the rush.

"Perfect." The Baron said.

My eyes met his.

Lord Ramsey swirled the blood, his wrist moving only slightly. He breathed in the scent of my blood.

I could taste the tang in the air, thought it might have been my imagination.

I silence grew heavy, and the anticipation was palpable.

The Baron tilted the glass and drank every precious drop of crimson. He pressed his lips together and closed his eyes. "My dear, it is better than I remember."

I was blushing. My face felt like it had caught fire and I wasn't sure why. I tore my eyes away from his face and busied myself with the bandage. When the knot was securely tied, I looked up again to find the Baron's face only a hair from mine.

"Delicious." His lips brushed my cheek.

My body froze as I felt his hand grip my knee. "You, you flatter me." I stammered.

"No, I only speak the truth."

I attempted to stand but his grip tightened. "We still have some time left," he said.

"Yes, but I'm afraid I can give no more blood tonight."

"I wasn't asking for blood." Lord Ramsey turned my head with his hand and crushed his lips against mine.

I gasped, throwing myself backwards and pulling myself out of his grasp. "You paid for my blood, not my body."

The Baron looked furious. His eyes glinted dangerously. "Do you forget yourself, Miss Violet?" He hissed.

My stomach dropped in fear. My blood stained the corner of his lips.

Lord Ramsey grabbed me again, forcing me down onto the chesterfield. "I'm not finished with you, girl." He growled.

"Does your wife know that this is what you do to Bloodletters?" I spat as I struggled in his grasp. He was much stronger than he looked.

The Baron laughed. "You're a funny girl," he said. "Smart too. So, you'll understand why girls like you never say no to me."

An idea clicked into place. "I wouldn't dream of saying no to you." I fluttered my eyelashes. "However, I feel like Madam might be unhappy if she found out about this."

The Baron's grip relaxed a fraction. "I won't tell her if you don't."

I gave him my best smile and kneed him in the gut. I heard a seam in my dress rip.

Lord Ramsey gasped for air. The shock twisted his handsome face into a caricature of what it used to be.

I pulled my arms free and pushed him away from me.

"You bitch!" He spat. "You'll regret that."

Without a second thought, I kicked, and my foot collided with his jaw.

He staggered backwards, holding his face.

"I won't tell her if you don't." I gasped before running out of the room as fast as I could.

NINE

"HOW ARE YOU FEELING?"

At lunch the next day I was the center of attention. The past week I had been kept busy with so much preparation that I had done little socializing. It was beginning to feel like home; I was used to living in a huge house without seeing members of my family for days on end.

Amelia sat beside me, asking how the first Bloodletting had gone.

"I'm ok," I replied. I hadn't mentioned the Baron's advances to Heather and judging by her neutrality towards me that morning, neither had he. My heart pounded every time I thought about what could have happened to me. In comparison, kicking a Royal in the face seemed like the best alternative.

"You look good," said the bearded man. His name was Thomas. He had been Bloodletting for three years. I had been surprised to know he was in his mid-twenties; this lifestyle had aged him dramatically.

I tried to smile. "Thanks."

"I heard you had twenty royals there," Greta spoke up. "At your Sampling." She clarified. "One of my clients attended." There was a hint of poison in her tone.

There had been so many names and faces that night I could scarcely remember. "Oh, really?" I mumbled.

"I'm not sure what your plan is, but keep your hands off of my clients," Greta said. She waved her fork around, pointing at the others. "Theirs too. We work hard for this. I'm not about to let you swoop in and undo all my efforts."

Thomas, Amelia, and Jack, the boy who always wore gloves, looked away awkwardly. No one seemed to ever want to confront Greta. I was mildly annoyed that no one came to my defense.

"I'm sorry if your clients are tired of the same old blood, maybe some variety will do them some good." I spat out the words before my conscious kicked in.

Greta's face flushed with rage. "How dare you!" She shrieked. She bolted to her feet and threw her fork down with a clang. "Do you have any idea how long I've been here? How much I've sacrificed for this?"

I clenched my teeth, biting back the flurry of angry retorts that came to mind.

Amelia held onto my sleeve. "Don't get her going, please, Violet," she whispered.

I exhaled and relaxed my shoulders. "I'm sorry, Greta. I don't know what came over me." My words sounded dead to me but seemed to appease her.

Greta smirked and sat down, smoothing her skirt. "Don't you worry Violet; you'll understand in time."

∞

The next morning, Heather met me in the hall. "Violet, may I speak to you for a second?"

My heart jumped in fear and my mouth went dry. Had the Baron told her what happened after all? "Yes?" I squeaked, holding back a million excuses that filled my chest to the point of bursting.

Heather had a bundle of envelops in her hand. She passed one to me. It was white and unmarked except with my name. "Your allowance from the Sampling."

I stared at the envelope. "But Madam said the wages were held."

Heather raised her eyebrows at me. "Do you not want the money?" She asked.

My grip tightened on the envelope. It was thick with the cash inside.

The woman laughed and shook her head. "Madam asked me to give you an advance so you could go shopping for clothes. Your appearance is second only to your blood, Miss Violet," she explained. "So,

Madam gives out small allowances once every month for you to use how you will."

I beamed. After all, I had been through, some retail therapy would be most effective. "Thank you."

Heather shook her head. "Don't thank me," she said. "I know Greta will go out today. I asked her to show you around. It is essential that Bloodletters don't wander the Capital alone."

My happiness deflated. "Greta?"

"Don't pout at me like that!" Heather shook her head. Her curls bounced and swayed. "I'm not your sitter. I may have been training you, but I still have to take care of everyone else. Besides, it will do you some good to get to know your housemates."

"Yes, ma'am." I grumbled.

That afternoon I met Greta in the foyer. She was dressed in a pastel pink dress and matching jacket. She had a parasol folded in her hand and her hair was tied up with white ribbons. Roger was dusting the mantel and making small talk with her.

I cleared my throat. "Good afternoon."

Greta glanced at me, looking at my burgundy dress. She wrinkled her nose. "Goodness, Violet, it's spring. Don't you have something more seasonal?"

"Well, I didn't really have time to pack before being kidnapped!" I shot back.

"Ladies!" Roger gasped. "Let's be civil, please."

Greta sighed and rolled her eyes. "I guess that's understandable," she said. "Well, come along."

Roger opened the door for us. "Do be careful, ladies."

"Yes Roger," Greta sang.

I followed Greta out the door and down the walkway. I had been to the market with Heather enough times to know the way on my own. Commoners such as ourselves, employees, and servants of the Royals normally staffed and frequented the stalls. Heather always made sure to point out influential Royals when we passed one, but for the most part, our trips to the market had always been unremarkable.

"I hope you plan on spending your allowance on a new wardrobe," Greta said. She was rushing through the streets.

I gritted my teeth. "Yes, that was what Heather suggested."

"What did Madam get you for your Sampling? What color did you wear?"

"Black."

"Ah, yes, classic. I was younger when I had my Sampling, so Madam picked soft pink for my color. That woman is a genius. I was full up with clients for weeks after that night!" Greta laughed.

We stopped for a carriage to cross the road before continuing. "How old were you?"

Greta shot me a look. "Why?"

I shrugged. "Just wondering."

"Twelve, if you must know," Greta answered.

I kept my reaction subdued. She looked to be in her early twenties, so I guessed that she must have been Bloodletting for ten years by now. "That's young," I mumbled.

Greta smirked. "Yes. I'll let you know that I am the most requested Bloodletter in the House now."

I remembered the night that Amelia and I had spied on her and there was no doubt in my mind that she was probably a favorite of the male clients. I shivered; raw memories of the Baron crept into my mind. I prayed that I never saw him again.

The clicking of Greta's heels on the cobblestone filled my ears. The streets were exceptionally bare for a Saturday. The tall buildings were crammed together as tightly as puzzle pieces. The streets were narrow and split at irregular intervals.

We turned a corner and entered the fashion district. The shop windows featured gowns in the same jewel tones that the women had worn to my Sampling. The Capital was further north and the warm weather was always short-lived. My mother had always taken her fashion queues based on what my father told her about the Capital. The Councilor's wives had whispered behind her back for wearing plum in July when they were dressed in lilac. I supposed that Greta's obsession with springtime colors might be attributed to where she was brought up.

A bright red gown in a window caught my attention. It was the most brilliant scarlet I had never seen in my life. I lingered, looking into the shop. A woman was there talking to the clerk. If I had to guess, the woman looked like a Royal. Her luxurious clothes and perfect posture were excellent clues.

The woman perked up and turned, feeling my gaze.

I gasped and stepped back. My heart shriveled at the predatory shine in her eyes.

"Come along Violet," Greta called without looking back.

I tore myself away from the window and ran a few paces to catch up with Greta.

"Try not to fall behind," Greta said. "Believe me, there are Royals who be more than happy to lead you astray."

We walked two more blocks before Greta came to a halt.

We stood in front of a dressmaker's shop, though it was much smaller than the others we had passed. The window was streaked with grime and the sign that hung above the door had faded beyond recognition.

I grimaced. "Here?"

Greta laughed. "Looks aren't everything." She opened the door, and a bell tinkled to announce our arrival.

Inside the narrow shop, there was a table and a few readymade garments hanging on a rail. The rest of the front room was filled with bolts of fabric nearly taller than me. Dusty floated through the air. I held my hand over my nose to prevent a sneeze.

"Ah, there's my favorite customer." I could hear a voice behind a pile of navy-blue velvet.

"Maurice," Greta said.

A frail old man emerged. His back was bent over in a permanent slouch. A pair of glasses dangled around his neck on a golden chair. "Greta, my angel, how are you?" He kissed her cheek.

"I am doing wonderfully."

Maurice caught sight of me. "Ah, and who is this lovely young lady?"

I waved nervously.

Greta spoke before I could open my mouth. "This is Violet, one of Madam's newest Bloodletters."

Maurice nodded and peered through his glasses. "Lovely, lovely. Madam Desjardins has some of the best in the Capital."

I tilted my head trying to figure out if he was a Royal or not. Some of them radiated power while others had felt as ordinary as me.

Greta rested a gentle hand on the man's shoulder. "She just came here, and she needs clothes."

Maurice nodded. "Leave it to me."

Three hours later, we left. With Greta's help, we selected fabrics, Maurice took my measurements and ordered five new dresses. I hoped that the old man was as skilled as Greta swore he was. I had left nearly all my allowance in that dusty shop at the end of the street.

"Really, wait until they get delivered." Greta gushed. "I mean, he made this one." She twirled in her pink dress. She had ordered another pink one too. "The details are just exquisite."

I nodded, not bothering to listen to her going on about the embroidery. While I had a rough idea of what was fashionable, it was not something I cared about. My entire life, my focus had been on learning politics and history. My mother had ensured I dressed well for social events but was always so focused on being the perfect heir that I never had time to look at fashion catalogues.

That gave me an idea. "Greta?"

"Yes?" She opened her parasol. The afternoon sun was growing hotter.

"Is there a bookstore nearby?" I asked. "Or anywhere that I could buy a newspaper?"

Greta wrinkled her nose. "Why would you want those? They just get your fingers all black."

I managed not to roll my eyes. "Well, before, I would read the paper to keep up with what was going on in the world."

"Oh, I forgot, you actually had a future ahead of you, didn't you?" Greta teased. "I forget, now that you're just like us."

I clenched my teeth and forced away my anger. I couldn't snap at her now because she knew how to get back to the House. "So, is there a place where I can buy the paper for Wythtir?"

Greta led me out of the fashion district and towards the main road. The buildings grew taller; a mix of banks, restaurants, and shops. There was a stall outside laden with newspapers from the Capital and the provinces. A skinny man sat on a stool sleeping. His mustache twitched as he snored.

I searched through the stacks of papers. One side of the cart was weighed down by publications from the Capital and the other side had papers from the provinces. As I scanned the dates, I realized that it had nearly been a month since my father had betrayed me. Over a month since my mother died.

I clenched a fist and slammed it down on a shelf.

The man snorted but didn't wake from his nap.

Greta sighed impatiently. "Hurry up, please."

The papers from Wythtir were closer to the bottom. My hands found a thick weekly digest. The headline reached out and slapped me across the face.

ACKERMAN FAMILY MOURNS DEATH OF HEIR.

TEN

I STARED INTO THE MIRROR. My skin was pale, and my hair had lost its sheen. I scrubbed the makeup off my eyes and lips with a sponge and dried my face with a soft towel. I shivered and wrapped a bathrobe around my body tightly.

I tiptoed down the hallway to my room. It was nearly dawn. Heather dragged me from my sleep to tend to a last-minute appointment. She and Madam had kept my schedule full the past two weeks. Draining me just shy of death as often as the Doctor would allow them.

I slipped into bed. Amelia was curled with her back towards me fast asleep. I pulled the quilt up around my shoulders and blew into my cold hands. I had never been so cold in all my life. It was May and though the weather was warm outside; the House kept the radiator on full blast.

I tossed and turned. Closed my eyes and stared at the ceiling or watched Amelia sleep. I was exhausted but couldn't rest.

With a groan, I rolled out of bed and pushed my feet into my slippers. I walked downstairs, avoiding the third step from the bottom that squeaked. I could smell coffee brewing and bread baking; I was not surprised to see the kitchen bustling with life. I sat by the hearth, warming myself by the fire and watching the pot of oatmeal bubbling.

Vincent turned, nearly dropping a pan of buns when he saw me. "Violet!" He gasped. "What are you doing up? There are no chores for you anymore, child."

I laughed bitterly. "No, only Bloodletting."

The cook's face softened. He set the pan down and pulled up a chair beside me. "What's eating you?" He smiled. "Besides the Royals, that is?"

I couldn't help chuckling at his dark humor. "Nothing, I just can't sleep."

"Famous last words." Vincent shook his head. The wooden chair creaked under his weight. "I know this is tough, but you have to stay strong."

I nodded.

"You're new, they always feed like crazy on fresh blood. But, don't worry, the novelty will wear off and it will slow down," he continued.

I rubbed my throbbing head. My hands felt like ice on my forehead. "How long have you been here?"

Vincent paused to think about it. "Oh Gods, Madam hired me the summer before Heather came, so just over twenty years now," He smiled and pulled the white cap from his head, revealing his baldness. "I know I look good for my age, but this helps hide evidence." He winked.

I smiled.

Vincent poured me some tea and went back to work.

I wrapped my hands around the mug and breathed in the steam. "Vincent," I asked. "What keeps you here?"

"Violet!" Heather's voice cut off his reply.

I jumped in my seat, managing not to drop the tea. "Yes?"

Heather emerged from the stairs the lead to the garden. She shut the door behind her and dusted off her apron. "What are you doing out of bed? I told you to sleep!"

"I can't sleep," I replied.

Heather narrowed her eyes at me. "You need your rest."

"You need to stop booking me appointments before I die!" I shot back.

Heather gritted her teeth, biting back whatever she wanted to say. She breathed in and out. "You won't die as long as you get your rest. Trust me, I've been at this for a while."

I looked away and took a sip of tea.

"Listen, I know you're having a hard time adjusting, but you should be grateful. You could have ended up in worse Blood Houses than this."

I made my way towards the stairs, clutching the mug with trembling hands. I looked over my shoulder at Heather. "A gilded cage is still a prison."

∞

Heather and I didn't speak for days. She escorted me to and from my appointments wordlessly.

On the third day of my self-imposed vow of silence, Heather cornered me after dinner.

"Violet." she said. I didn't know when she had dropped the formalities, but she spoke to me as if she was as familiar with me as she was with Vincent.

I turned and waited for her to continue.

"You think you have it pretty hard here, huh?" She asked with her hands on her hips.

I heard the clattering of flatware as the maid, Miss Prescott, cleared the table.

I raised my chin, my lips sealed.

I expected Heather to get angry, furious even, with my childish resistance. She only sighed and shook her head. "Come with me."

I hesitated.

"Come," Heather commanded.

Something in her tone made me comply. I followed her to the foyer, managing to keep my silence even when she handed me a long coat. Roger was missing from his usual post by the front door. I pulled on the coat and followed her outside.

Heather walked quickly. Her face was nearly concealed by the shadow cast by her hat. She said nothing to me and did not glance over her shoulder to make sure I was following.

The sun was setting, the buildings spilled long shadows over the cobblestone street. I followed a few paces behind her. As we walked, the buildings became shorter and in obvious disrepair. In the few times I had ventured out of the House, we had always walked east to the markets. Now we were walking west with the blood red sun blazing in the distance.

Horse carriages rolled past us and pedestrians stared just long enough to give me chills. I dashed a few steps to catch up with her.

"Where are we going?" I couldn't hold my silence any longer.

"You'll see," Heather said.

I glared at the back of her head and glanced around. The surrounding houses were slanted and slouched. Broken glass from windows littered the ground. The yowling of stray cats filled the air. I had never witnessed such poverty before in all my life. My nose wrinkled at a pungent smell of rotten food and urine. I held my sleeve to my nose.

Just as I was going to try to convince Heather to turn around, she stopped.

We were standing in front of a two-story building with a slanted roof. The front bottom windows were boarded up, but the top was lit up. There was noise coming from inside. The building was nondescript except for a red lantern hanging above the door.

I swallowed the lump in my throat. "What is this place?"

A loud bang echoed down the lane beside us and a skinny white cat shot down the street.

"You don't like your gilded cage?" Heather whispered. "Do you want to see what a real prison looks like?"

The sky was growing dark above us and the breeze brought in a chill. I wrapped my arms around myself. "No, no, that's ok. Let's go back, please."

Heather smirked. "Too late, Violet." Without warning, she grabbed my wrist and pulled me down the dark alley.

I pulled against her, but she was stronger than she looked.

A window down the side of the building was open. I could hear laughter and voices talking. The stench of rotten meat drifted into my nose and I covered my face with my hand again. If Heather noticed the smell, she didn't say anything about it.

Heather nodded her head towards the basement window. "Look."

I braced myself and peeked in the window. There were people inside a tiny room with hardly any furniture. A woman who was barely dressed was speaking to a man with a familiar glint in his eye. In the corner were two men passed out and dressed in stained clothes. Another woman was by the door, swaying and looking at her hands.

The man grinned as the scantily clad woman held her arm up. She picked up a dagger from the floor and sliced into her skin.

I choked back a gasp and tried to turn my head. Heather's hand was on my neck, immobilizing me. I shut my eyes tightly instead.

"Watch, Violet. Consider this your most important lesson."

I forced my eyes open to see the man drinking blood directly from the woman's arm. She was pale and riddled with bruises. Her eyes were sunken into her skull. She smiled and swayed as the Royal drank her blood.

The buzzing of flies in my ear couldn't drown out the sounds of her laughing hysterically. Her eyes were glazed as if someone had drugged her. The man released her arm, and she sank to the dirty floor.

Finally, Heather let me go.

I gasped and sank down onto the ground. I held back tears, hiccupping and trying to catch my breath.

I heard shouts from inside the slanted building. Heather grabbed me and pulled me into the shadows. I put my hand over my mouth to keep silent.

More shouting and the door slammed again. A man stumbled out, stared down the alley and shuffled off.

I sighed and sat on the ground, abandoning any dignity I had left. I held my hand to my chest, feeling my pounding heart. "Is this a Blood House?"

Heather snorted. "If you can call it that," she said. "Royals come to places like this to get their kicks. It let their demons loose for a little while."

I shivered, remembering the Baron. My other clients had been polite, respectful, and not very talkative. Strictly business. I was suddenly grateful for their restraint. I relaxed against the side of the building and let my hands fall to my sides.

The flies buzzing was overwhelming. My hand brushed something cold. I glanced down and, in the shadows, saw a human hand a strange shade of blue. I bolted to my feet, clapping my hands over my mouth again. My wide eyes unable to move away from the body. It was a woman; her face rotted beyond recognition.

Heather caught me as I reeled backwards. She kept a tight hold on my arm and pulled me from the alley. Walked as quickly as possible without attracting attention. I muffled my sobs, biting down on my lip until I tasted blood.

I finally collapsed on a bench when we reached a safe distance.

Heather looked shaken but kept her voice steady. "I'm sorry. I didn't realize." She whispered.

I gagged and threw up, keeping my head between my knees, not caring when the contents of my stomach splattered against my boots.

Heather handed me a flask of water from her coat pocket.

I drank deeply and closed my eyes, unable to get the memory of the woman's rotting face out of my head.

Heather sat beside me and took off her hat. She ran her fingers through her tightly coiled hair and sighed. "I didn't mean for that to happen," she said. "I just wanted to show you what could have happened if Madam hadn't signed your contract."

I snorted and shook my head. "Lesson learned," I muttered, hugging my arms around myself. A passing carriage broke the silence. "How did you know about that place?" My voice was raspy.

Heather looked at her hands. "That's where I was before Madam found me."

For a moment, I didn't believe her. "You?" I gasped.

Heather nodded. "Yes." She shrugged. "Not long, though, thank the Gods. When I was fourteen, a man came to my father, this was back in my home country," she added. "We were poor, and he told my father that

112

the Royals would love a beautiful dark-skinned girl as a servant. He promised security and good pay. He agreed, and they sent me to the Capital. Now, even to this day, I believe that the man was telling the truth. He worked for the highest nobility, looking for exotic blood. But when we arrived, I was kidnapped and brought here."

She gestured down the way we had run. She looked at her hands for a moment before continuing. "Thankfully, Madam always has her ears open for new Bloodletters. She found out about me and bought me shortly after that. Then I had a proper Sampling, a list of clients and, most importantly, given a home and treated with respect."

I rubbed my hands together to warm them. "I see," I said. "I'm sorry, if I would have known, I wouldn't have –"

"Don't worry." Heather cut me off. "Nothing will change the past. I just wanted to teach you how lucky you are to have Madam."

"And you," I added.

Heather sniffed and shook her head. "I guess so."

"Can I ask you something?" I looked up. The sky was dark now, brightened by a crescent moon and twinkling stars.

"What?"

"Why do you stay?"

"With Madam?" Heather sounded surprised. "Well, I'm the mentor. It's my job to train new Bloodletters."

"Yes, but twenty years? Haven't you cheated death long enough?" I looked at her. "You could have gone home."

"The Blood House is my home."

I didn't argue. There was no point.

"Maybe," Heather said. "It will be your home, too."

"Not for long," I said.

She chuckled. "You sound determined."

"As soon as I'm a legal adult, I'm gone," I said, clenching my cold hands.

Heather nodded. "Then that's your choice." She paused. "I saw the headlines, you know. You'll find there's peace in being dead."

ELEVEN

I WAS DEAD.

Part of me felt strangely relieved. I sat on my bed with the front page of the newspaper in my hands. I read the article over and over. I must have read it a thousand times. The thin paper was wrinkled and smeared with ink.

It was wonderfully written, telling the story of a family had only begun to heal from the loss of a mother and wife, only to have their daughter disappear on a boating trip. Her body had not been found, and she was presumed to have drowned.

I shook my head. How convenient. What the article had not mentioned was that the father had sold his daughter for her blood. And that she was a great swimmer.

There was a peaceful side of being dead. No more expectations, no family name to tie me to and no history. Here I was, Violet. Just plain Violet. No, not plain, I decided. I could start new. And I would not waste this chance.

∞

From that night on, I didn't waste a single moment pouting or whining or getting angry. Every time I felt my mood begin to sour, I closed my eyes and imagined the dead Bloodletter left to rot in the alley.

The dresses I ordered from Maurice finally arrived and I was not disappointed. Two in black, one a robin's egg blue, a mint green, and a rich red. They all had full skirts, cinched in waists and low necklines, as was the fashion for the Capital – according to Greta. I dressed in darker colors for my evening appointments, lighter for my daytime ones.

My schedule remained busy but not as full as the first two weeks. Thankfully, I had not seen the Baron since my first Bloodletting. My other appointments had been uneventful, and I was getting much better at the entire Bloodletting process.

I rested well and ate my fill at every meal. The doctor was happy with my health and hadn't removed me from the roster yet. Amelia was on bedrest often. As for the others, I didn't know, because we kept conversation light and casual during meals.

May rolled into June, bringing long days and hot weather. The amount of appointments slowed to a trickle.

At dinner one night, I mentioned it, worrying that it was only my clients that had tapered off. "Does the amount of appointments change based on the season?"

Thomas looked up from his plate of liver and onions. "What do you mean?"

I hesitated, hoping I wasn't the only one experiencing a lull in appointments. I felt their eyes on me. "Well, I found business has slowed down a bit."

Thomas nodded. "Lots of Royals go north to their vacation homes when the weather gets too hot." He took a bite of bread.

Greta smirked. "Those who can afford to anyway," she added, daintily picking at her meal. "It's terrible for Bloodletters like me who host the best of the best, knowing they're getting their blood from somewhere else."

Jack, the boy with gloves, rolled his eyes. "It's not always about you."

I stared. He barely ever spoke.

Amelia gasped beside me. This was her first meal with the rest of the house in a week. She was having trouble recouping and the lull in business would no doubt serve her well.

Greta glared at Jack.

The tension in the room was high. Apparently, I wasn't the only one worried about the lack of business.

As if reading my mind, Thomas spoke up. "Don't worry. They'll be back in the fall. We should enjoy the rest."

Penelope, the girl who was always buried in sweaters spoke in her tiny voice. "I know I appreciate the break."

Greta pouted and pushed her plate away. "If not giving blood is something you all celebrate, maybe you are in the wrong line of work." She spat and stood.

No one called after her as she left. We sat in silence for a while. Tea and brownies were served for dessert.

Thomas glanced around the quiet table. "Oh, come on now, everyone," he said around a mouthful. "Don't let her get to you. She's just sore because a Collection is coming up."

I set down my teacup. "Collecting?"

Thomas nodded. "The ultimate goal, for a Bloodletter like her," he explained. "The highest Royals and the ruling family request blood samples from the most exclusive Blood Houses. Then, if they taste blood that they like, they will buy out the contract from the owner of the House. Then that Bloodletter will become private property."

I frowned. "Why would Greta want that?"

"To be a personal Bloodletter to a Royal?" Jack peeped. "Just imagine the luxury. A private room, no line of clients, living in a mansion or a chateau." His voice went soft. "That's right up her alley. She's a princess in her own mind, after all."

The rest of the table nodded in agreement.

"And another thing," Thomas added. "Greta's been here so long and never been Collected. She takes it personally. So, maybe steer clear from her until the Collection is over."

I leaned back in my chair, leaving my brownie untouched. "I see."

Amelia patted my hand. "Don't worry, you're too new, they won't be Collecting from you."

A strange feeling settled in my gut. Disappointment?

∞

When Dr. Coleman came to take samples from the more experienced Bloodletters, I sat alone in the parlor and waited.

"Feeling left out?" Roger was cleaning again. I doubted even a speck of dust could hit the floor without him hearing it.

I shrugged and curled my legs underneath me. I was sitting in a green wingback chair by a window that presented a beautiful view of the gardens.

"Don't worry, Miss Violet," he said. "You'll have your chance soon enough."

I forced a smile and looked out the window. Bees were flitting from one flower to the next. I couldn't explain why I felt disappointed. I had just begun to adjust to this new life; the last thing I should want was a change. Yet, that was what I craved the most.

Amelia entered the parlor with a sigh and sunk onto the sofa opposite me. A fresh bandage was tied around her arm. She pulled a blanket around her legs.

"How was it?" I asked.

Amelia shrugged. Her round eyes were watery and tired. "The usual. They don't take much, but there is paperwork and health forms to fill out."

"They're so strict," I said.

"Well, death from diseased blood is close to the King's heart. It's how his father died after all," Roger said.

"Your blood goes straight to the King?" I asked.

"Well, the ruling family gets the first pick and then the other nobility picks from what's left," Amelia said. She shivered. "I hope I get passed over again."

"The way Jack talked about it, it sounded like being Collected would be a charmed life," I replied. "For a Bloodletter anyway."

"Oh, it would." Greta sat down beside Amelia. She fidgeted with the bandage around her arm. "Being a Bloodletter for a Prince." She threw her head back in a swoon. "Now that's a life."

"It's a life sentence, more like," Amelia muttered.

"Like you're going to accomplish anything better?" Greta shot back. "Save your money, find your true love and live happily ever after?" She sneered.

Amelia looked away and bit her nails. The slightest pink tinge shone in her cheeks.

I glared at the blond. "Don't mock her dream."

"Oh, pardon me!" She laughed.

I gritted my teeth. "You know, I can see why you never get Collected. If I were a Royal, I bet your blood would make me sick."

Greta's beautiful face contorted with anger. "How dare you!" She shrieked. Without warning, she leaped towards me like a wild animal. She tackled me against the chair, slapping my face.

"Ladies!" Roger shouted, dropping his duster.

Amelia cried out. "Stop it, Greta!"

I shoved her back, clawing at her with the same ferocity. All my pent-up anger and frustration came rushing out.

Strong hands pulled us apart and Thomas shoved himself between us. "Violet! Greta!" He boomed.

Greta took a step back, breathing hard. "She started it!"

"I did not!" I screamed back.

"I don't care who started it!" Thomas hissed. "Stop acting like children."

I plopped down on the sofa beside Amelia. She was starting at me with her round eyes, terrified. I looked away, ashamed of my outburst.

"What's going on in here?" Heather stormed into the room.

I didn't meet her eyes.

Greta pointed at me, but Thomas quickly slapped her hand away.

Heather glared at us in turn. "There's a representative from the government here with Dr. Coleman, I'm sure I need not remind you of the severity of the Collections." She hissed at us. "Keep it down in here, or you'll answer to me." She slammed the door behind her as she left.

Thomas let out a breath he was holding in.

Greta choked out a sob, hiding her face with her hand. She had scratch marks on her arm. I had done that.

I had never physically attacked anyone in anger before. I looked at the red lines on her arm and clenched my fists.

Roger cleared his throat. I had forgotten he was there. "I think," he said. "I think I'll put on a pot of tea."

∞

Over two weeks passed when the results of the Collecting came back. It had been a relatively quiet two weeks with few clients and lots of rest. My cold hands and feet were warming up, my skin was looking healthier and the weight I had lost was coming back slowly.

Amelia told me to enjoy the lull. Winter was the longest season for a Bloodletter. Hungry clients, lack of sunshine and absence of fresh fruit and vegetables made recovery hard.

Amelia and I were sitting in the garden when the news arrived. Amelia was trying to teach me a card

122

game common in Chwetir, where she grew up, but I couldn't get the hang of it. Not to mention that the wind was adding an extra level of difficulty.

She was giggling and I couldn't help but stare at her. This was the first time I could remember having a friendship with a girl my age. The girls I met at balls and made small talk with, I used to hold on to those conversations and pretend that they were my friends, but I was only a rung in the social ladder. They agreed with me to win favor and investigate me for their brothers who only saw me as a political conquest.

Amelia snorted and blushed. She had only seen two clients this past while and her health was returning as well.

I smiled, appreciating the moment.

"Good afternoon, ladies." Roger approached with a tray of tea and scones. He set it down on the table between us.

"Hello, Roger," Amelia said. "I'm trying to teach her Five Fingers."

Roger laughed. "Oh, that one." He winked at me. "She tried to teach me last winter when we were snowed in by a dreadful blizzard. If I must say, it's better with more than two players."

Amelia waved her hand. "She needs to learn the basics before she embarrasses herself in front of Thomas."

"Is Thomas from Chwetir too?" I asked.

Amelia shook her head and tightened the ribbon around her ponytail. "No, but he is a lover of card games."

Roger poured us tea and then pulled an envelope from his jacket pocket. "This came for you, Miss Amelia. About the Collection."

Amelia blanched. She took the envelope with trembling hands. She read the letter quickly, her eyes flicking back and forth wildly, before letting out a sigh and falling back in her chair. "Denied. Thank the Gods."

Roger nodded. "Glad to hear it. So, we won't be losing anyone this season." He bowed his head. "I'll see you at dinner, ladies."

I watched as Amelia crumpled up the paper and threw it into the fountain. "I guess that means Greta will be staying with us too?"

Amelia rolled her eyes. "Unfortunately." She gasped and pressed her fingers to her lips. "That was not kind of me."

I couldn't help but laugh.

TWELVE

LADY BENEDICT WAS ONE OF MY FAVORITE
CLIENTS. She returned from her holiday early due to
her husband's urgent business matters. The Countess
was always reserved, quiet, and patient as one would
expect a lady of her station.

She sipped my blood and made polite talk while
she drank. She was most interested in my upbringing,
but I never revealed my family name, only that I had
grown up with the nobility of Wythtir. She asked many
questions but seemed satisfied with weak answers.

When our time together was done, I bowed my
head to her. The Countess thanked me for my company
before leaving.

As I left, I caught a glance of myself in the mirror and paused to adjust the mint green dress. I smoothed it over my hips and straightened the bodice.

There was a knock at the door.

"Yes?" I called.

"It's just me." It was Heather. She opened the door. "You hadn't come out, so I was worried."

I waved away her worries. "Fine, just needed a moment to myself." I collected the Bloodletting tools and handed them to her for sterilization.

"Great, I'll see you at dinner then," She said. "Oh, and happy Summer Festival."

I startled, realizing the date. The first day of summer and a holiday for all the provinces. The people of Wythtir were celebrating with parties, buffets and drunken dancing. My heart fluttered with a hint of homesickness. I buried the feeling deep inside myself and carried on.

∞

Dinner was perfect as always, with red meat and an assortment of vegetables and side dishes. Thomas, Penelope, Jack, and Amelia were there. Greta was in her room sulking from yet another rejection to be Collected.

"She'll come around," Thomas said with a shrug.

"It's been three days, how much time does she need?" Penelope said. She was wrapped up in only one beige sweater that night. "I mean, after ten years, isn't it obvious that they're not interested?"

"It's not necessarily that her blood is bad; there just might be better options in other Houses."

"No." I slipped into the conversation. "I'm pretty sure her blood is just spoiled."

The others stifled laughs.

Heather walked in with a large chocolate cake decorated with white icing and enormous strawberries. "Who's ready for dessert?"

We gasped as one. The others turned to Amelia and grinned. "Happy Birthday!"

Amelia squealed and buried her face in her hands to hide her face. "Oh, you didn't have to." She mumbled.

Heather set down the cake between us. Miss Prescott cleared away the dinner plates as silently as a ghost. Vincent stuck his head around the corner. "Do you like it?"

Amelia turned a brighter shade of red. "It's perfect, thank you."

"Hey, it's not every day a girl turns seventeen." Vincent winked before heading back to the kitchen.

I smiled at her. Two more years and she would take her savings and go back to get married and start a life. I admired her for her goals.

I was still in limbo.

∞

The next morning, I didn't feel like my normal self. The puncture wound from my meeting with the

127

Countess was red and throbbing. I rolled over and groaned.

Amelia was sitting on the edge of her bed, brushing her long hair. "What's wrong, Violet?"

I shook my head. "It's nothing," I said. I inspected my arm discretely. There was a large purplish bruise where I had inserted the needle yesterday and the skin was especially tender. I went over the steps in my head and I knew I had taken care of the wound properly after the appointment.

I excused myself to the washroom and pressed a cold wet cloth against the burning skin. I dug fresh bandages from a basket on the wall and wrapped my arm tightly.

By that evening, I felt as if I were running a fever. I laid on my bed in my nightgown; the cotton stuck to my skin. I shivered uncontrollably.

Heather's distinctive knock woke me from a restless nap. "Violet?"

My parched mouth struggled to form words. "Yes?" I croaked.

The bedroom door flew open and Heather rushed to my side. "Violet! Are you ok?" She dropped to her knees and felt my forehead.

I tried to speak, but the words came out in an indistinguishable wheeze.

Heather seized my right arm and ripped off the bandage. The tiny wound was red and leaking puss.

"Infection!" She hissed and hauled me to my feet. "You need to see the doctor now."

I nodded and allowed myself to be led down the stairs to Dr. Coleman's office. I was dizzy and nauseous by the time we stopped.

Heather rapped on the door. "Doctor!" She called.

The doctor opened the door and raised his eyebrows. "Yes?"

Heather pushed past him and helped me onto the cot. "She has an infection in her right arm."

Dr. Coleman inspected the swollen wound and tutted. "Yes, that's what it looks like. Lucky you caught her when you did."

"She had an appointment later, I came to get her," Heather said. She gasped and snapped her fingers. "I must arrange a replacement. Excuse me, doctor."

Dr. Coleman waved her off. He held my arm up to the light and pressed on the bruise.

I winced.

He wet a towel and placed it on my burning forehead. "Don't worry, Miss Violet," he said. "I'll fix you up and you'll be right as rain in no time." He rummaged through his tools. The doctor sliced into the wound with a scalpel and squeezed the pus out. I didn't even so much as whine until he pressed an alcohol-soaked cloth to the cut.

The doctor wiped the cut and patted it dry before wrapping it with a fresh bandage. "There you go." He said. "You'll have to keep an eye on it." He went to his cabinet and returned with a tincture. He poured some into a paper cup and handed it to me. "This will help with the pain."

I drank it quickly and grimaced at the taste. "How did this happen? I've always taken good care of my wounds."

Dr. Coleman shook his head. "Even all the precautions in the world won't stop an infection now and then." He took off his glasses and wiped them on the hem of his white coat. "Bloodletters have several challenges to face, health wise," he continued. "Your immune system is under constant pressure, so the occasional infection should be expected."

I nodded and took the cold compress away from my head.

"Now all you need to do is rest," The doctor said with a stern look. "I'll have to check your blood in a few days to see if it is fit to be ingested."

Heather returned to help me to my room. She closed the blinds tightly and tucked me into bed.

"You don't have to do this." I murmured.

Heather shook her head. "Of course, I do. I'm the house mentor."

I rubbed my eyes. "Why?"

Heather looked puzzled. "What do you mean, why?"

"Why do you do all this? A Bloodletter, a mentor, Madam's assistant, half the maid's work," I could have gone on, but my mouth was too dry.

Heather smiled and shook her head. "I thought you would have realized this was my life now, Violet." She said, smoothing my hair back from my forehead with care. "For some people, the thought of being a Bloodletter for life seems crazy, stupid even. The average lifespan of a Bloodletter is twenty-two, based on a starting age of fifteen. Playing with fire, I believe the saying goes," She said.

I nodded, trying to keep my eyes open. The medicine the doctor gave me was making me sleepy.

"Besides, Madam is nearing the end of her lifespan," Heather said quietly. "No one is immortal, not even the Royals. She has to give the House to someone."

"What do you mean?" I blinked a few times. My voice was weak.

Heather smiled, staring off into space. "It's rumored that commoners can become Royal, though the science is weak, and experiments are inconsistent," she whispered. "I've given my blood to them for twenty years. They can give me some of theirs."

THIRTEEN

"I'VE GIVEN MY BLOOD TO THEM FOR TWENTY YEARS. THEY CAN GIVE ME SOME OF THEIRS."

I believed that Heather only spoke to me that way, thinking I'd be too drugged to remember, but I couldn't forget a word.

The infection passed and I was cleared to begin Bloodletting the week after.

The summer swept in a blazing heat that I could barely feel in my frozen hands and feet. The days and nights passed slowly, and I fell into a complacent rhythm of bleeding, eating, and recovery.

"Amelia," I said to her one day as we were lounging in the garden. The doctor was convinced that spending time in the sun would be good for us.

Amelia shaded her eyes from the sun with the book she was reading. "Yes?"

I shut the book in my lap. We had started a miniature reading club to pass the slow summer months. She was a slow reader, so I often had to hold comments for a day or two, waiting for her to catch up. "I was just thinking," I continued. "It's been four months since I came here and there's only still the six of us at dinner, when the table could easily sit more. Why has there not been any new Bloodletters?"

Amelia hesitated, and I wondered if it were a more appropriate question for Heather. As much as I appreciated Heather for what she did, I knew that she told me half-truths. Amelia, when she spoke, seemed to be more reliable.

"Well," Amelia started. She set her book down and took a sip of lemonade. "It's a slow season, with all the Royals being on vacation. Besides that, I think Madam is very choosy with whom she hires."

I asked the question that had been burning my tongue for days. "Do you think she just took me in to replace Rose?"

Amelia paled and looked away. No one ever spoke of Rose, who had died only weeks before my arrival. No other names of dead Bloodletters grazed their lips. Even speaking of Greta's former roommate Beatrice, who had retired healthy and very much alive, was taboo.

"Maybe," she whispered.

I wanted to regret my words that made her eyes swim with tears, but I couldn't. On the outside I did everything that was expected of me: Bloodletting almost daily with no complaint of exhaustion or sickness. Inside, Heather's words rang like booming temple bells.

∞

July passed into August, and August faded into September, and the business began to pick up again. The days grew cooler and the nights longer; my schedule began to fill. Back-to-back Bloodletting appointments were exhausting, and I was thankful that I had recovered my strength over the summer.

One evening in mid-September I was called to an unexpected appointment. I was tired, nearly too tired to put on a smile as I climbed the stairs and followed Heather to the small rooms on the third floor.

Heather gestured to the first room. "This is your last appointment for the evening, please make sure you join us for dinner after."

I nodded, and she left me. When I opened the door, a small sound of surprise escaped my lips and my skin went cold.

Lord Ramsey was sitting there, looking as fearsome and calm as ever.

I let a mask of pleasant indifference slide over my face. "Good evening," I said as I shut the door behind me.

The Royal smiled. "Hello. Your beauty has only grown since last time we met."

I clenched my teeth. How dare he show his face in this Blood House again? I had never reported his inappropriate actions towards me, and he had not filed a complaint against me either. I had been led to believe we were in some sort of silent treaty and I would never have to give him my blood again. I was wrong.

Lord Ramsey looked me up and down and then motioned to the chair beside him. "Well, are you just going to stand by the door all night while I starve?"

I bit back a snide remark. Instead, I silently sat down and prepared my Bloodletting tools. I kept myself focused on the needles and tubing as to not make eye contact with him. I could feel him looking at me.

"You're blushing," he whispered and reached out to me. He wrapped one of my curls around his finger. "Have you missed me? I apologize for not returning sooner. I had business in the North, you see."

I turned my face from him and cleared my throat. "Quite alright. Which arm, sir?" I kept my tone business-like. I did not want him getting any ideas.

"The lady's choice." Lord Ramsey purred.

I used the opportunity to pull away from him and draw the blood. I didn't miss his breathing in my ear as the blood flowed. He was positively repulsive. I could not see the handsomeness of his face anymore. He was nothing but a monster to me.

I gave him the glass without a word and quickly concealed the wound.

Lord Ramsey drank the blood quickly. He grinned and smacked his lips. "You are as delicious as ever, my dear."

I wanted to run away. "Thank you, sir," I said with all the false politeness I could muster. "Now, if that's everything, I should be going. I am expected at dinner." I added, so he knew there would be consequences if I went missing.

The man put his hand on my knee, and I flinched away. He grabbed my thigh harder. "So soon? But I haven't seen you in almost a lifetime. Can't you stay with me a moment longer?"

I shuddered. "I'm sorry sir, but I must be going."

"I said *stay*!" Lord Ramsey grabbed my hand and twisted.

I pulled away, his grip ripping off my amber ring. It spun away on the hardwood floor and bounced under the radiator. A scream erupted from my throat.

"Hush, beautiful." He grabbed my shoulders. His eyes blazed as his Royal strength overpowered me. He wrestled me to the floor. "Such a pretty, delicious little morsel." He hissed. He kicked open my legs and kneeled between them.

I screamed again, fighting and clawing with all of my might. My efforts were in vain.

My skin crawled as he kissed my neck. "Why don't you say that we do this the old-fashioned way, hm?"

He grinned. He ripped open the top buttons of my dress, exposing more pale skin.

Suddenly, the door burst open and Lord Ramsey was on his feet in a flash.

Madam Desjardins was standing in the doorway. Vincent was behind her; for the first time his large frame looked dangerous rather than jolly. He was nearly as wide as the door frame with his shoulders squared.

"What is going on here?" Madam demanded.

I scrambled away from the Lord, trying to stifle my panicked sobs.

"Nothing!" Lord Ramsey shouted defensively.

Heather swept past Madam Desjardins and took me in her arms. I hadn't noticed the tears running down my cheeks until she wiped them away. She glared at Ramsey and pulled me to her chest.

"Get out of my House," Madam said with controlled anger. She was seething, but her Royal poise and dignity did not waiver.

"I did nothing!"

Vincent cracked his knuckles. If there was any mortal alive who I thought stood a chance against a Royal, it was him. His meaty hands balled into fists at his sides. "You heard her. Get out!" He barked.

I closed my eyes as Lord Ramsey stalked out of the small room. Vincent and Madam followed him.

Heather held me to her chest and rocked back and forth slowly, humming a song I didn't know. She whispered in a language that I could only assume was her native tongue. It was soft and soothing.

In the safety of her arms, I could almost feel my mother's love again. I let out a choking sob as the grief overtook me. It was supposed to get easier. Mourning was supposed to fade. But since coming to this Gods forsaken place, I hadn't had a moment to miss my mother.

Heather rubbed small circles on my back as I wept. "It's ok, Violet," she whispered. "Let it out." Then she resumed her calming foreign song.

For the first time in months, I pushed my strength aside and allowed myself to grieve.

FOURTEEN

AT MIDNIGHT ON MY EIGHTEENTH BIRTHDAY, I
BREATHED A PRAYER. "One more year of this, then I
will be my own master." The clock chimed in
agreement.

My client had already left. He drank my blood
quickly and wordlessly. I was left alone to clean the
wound and wrap it.

My birthday was the day before the Autumn
Festival, so all the Royals had other things on their
mind.

According to Heather, the Autumn Festival was the
second biggest holiday in the Capital. While we
commoners seemed to revel in the celebrations that

139

welcomed the beginning of warmer months, the Royals preferred the coldness of the other half of the year.

After I bandaged my wound, and tidied my tools, I left the room and went downstairs. The House was eerily quiet, my appointment had been the last of the day.

Heather met me in the hall and took the black bag of tools from me. "Happy Birthday, Violet," she said with a smile.

"Thank you," I said.

There was a click and a hiss from the radiator under the window.

"One more thing before you sleep?" Heather asked.

"What is it?" I replied, hoping to the Gods that there was not a last-minute client. The sudden influx in Royals had left me weak and tired.

Heather shook her head. "There is a charity ball tomorrow after the Autumn Festival parade," she explained. "Now there has been an unfortunate health violation in the House that was going to provide Bloodletters, so Madam has graciously stepped forward and offered some of ours."

I gritted my teeth. Sometimes I forgot that I was owned by that woman. "Yes." I said to her unasked question. "I would be happy to attend if she needs me."

Heather breathed a sigh of relief. "Good, I was hoping you would say that. Penelope is too weak, and Amelia is currently, ahem, unclean." Heather whispered. "It would be improper to send her, you see."

I nodded. Female Bloodletters never worked during their womanly time.

"Greta and Thomas will join us, and I will escort you," Heather continued. "Madam is attending as an esteemed guest, but please act as if you've never met. It is important that the guests do not know which Blood House is supplying the blood, to avoid gossip."

I nodded again.

Heather patted my shoulder. "Thank you, Violet," she said. "Now go get some rest."

∞

With the excitement of the Autumn Festival, my birthday went widely unnoticed to all except Vincent, who cut me an extra-large slice of shortcake with my afternoon tea.

The next day, the Capital burst to life. Royals were out dressed in their finest and music filled the streets. The Royals dressed in autumn colors: rich reds, bright oranges and bold yellows popped in the gray city.

I sat by the window in the parlor, watching them pass. It was barely past noon, and the gala began at nine. The waiting was killing me.

Greta sat on the sofa filing her fingernails. She was more excited and animated than I had ever seen her before. She had twisted her hair elegantly on top of her head, lined her eyes, rouged her cheeks and moisturized every inch of her visible skin. Her perfume could be smelled a mile away.

I sighed, and she tutted at me. "Why the long face, Violet?" She asked, pausing to examine her nails. "I can barely sit still."

"I noticed." I tried to keep the bite out of my voice.

Greta swung her legs off the sofa and stood. "Seriously?" She spat. "You can't tell me you're not even the littlest bit interested? The best of the best will be at that ball, the richest, most influential Royals of the country."

I looked at her. She wore a beautiful gown of gold brocade silk, her corset pulled so tight I doubted that she could breathe comfortably. I hadn't changed or readied myself in any way, not wanting to risk dirtying the beautiful red dress that Heather had given me that morning. "Why do you enjoy Bloodletting so much, Greta?"

Greta looked taken aback. "Why do you seem to hate it?"

"You didn't answer my question."

Greta's eyes darkened. "You wouldn't understand."

"Try me," I replied. I shifted in the window seat to face her fully.

The blond sat back down on the sofa and sighed. "If you really must know," she hesitated, twisting her pinky finger nervously. "It's because I've never been good at much else."

Her answer surprised me. "That's not true," I said. "You're excellent at playing the piano." I rattled off, remembering how well she played in the parlor at night. Her music filled the House during the quiet summer months. "And you're," I struggled to find another aspect of her I enjoyed.

Greta waved her hand to silence me. "Don't spare me, Violet," she said. "Everything I am, I owe to Madam. I'm too old to be married off without a sizeable dowry. Besides, I've learned to enjoy this independent life I live."

So that was what she got out of this, freedom. Bloodletting liberated her and left her control of her own destiny. That resonated within me in a way that I found hard to describe and I found myself, for the first time, agreeing with her.

"Now you answer me," Greta demanded.

An honest answer would require me to dig up all the emotions I had buried. I wasn't prepared to hurt again. I laughed her question off. "What makes you think I don't enjoy it?"

Greta raised her eyebrows. "Despite what our housemates might think, I'm not stupid."

I looked away. "Fine," I sighed. I struggled to find an answer that would appease her so she would go back to preening and leave me alone. "I'm still adjusting to this new life and the thought of being in a room filled with Royals again..." I trailed off and shivered. I could

143

only hope that Lord Ramsey would not be in attendance.

∞

"Here, put this on." Heather handed me a glittering red mask. It was the same shocking scarlet as my dress.

My hands froze midway. "Why?"

Heather shoved it into my hand. "Because I say so." Her calm demeanor had changed to the snappy one that I hadn't seen since my Bloodletter training.

The half mask sparkled in my hands. I looked down at it before lifting it to my face and tying the gold ribbon at the back of my head.

Heather adjusted my hair to hide the knot.

We had come to the venue by carriage. One of the Royal families was hosting the event in a grand ballroom. A servant ushered in us through a backdoor and sat in a room beside the kitchen. The smells and sounds of cooking leaked under the door.

Greta took a gold mask from Heather and put it on. Thomas' mask was black to match his suit.

Another mentor was tending to his staff of Bloodletters on the other side of the room. Heather had warned us against mingling with the competition. Here, we were to be civil and work together, but once the ball was over, our Houses would be rivals once more. I had never imagined how competitive the high-end Blood Houses were until then.

Heather fixed her own mask. She was dressed in a demure shade of burgundy to avoid attention. She would not be Bloodletting tonight.

"How many Royals are attending?" Greta asked in a hushed voice.

"At least two hundred. This is a very important event. Many business deals and marriage arrangements will be made tonight."

I noticed Greta's cheeks flush with anticipation.

"Ok," Heather sighed. Her hands were shaking nervously. "Let's go over the rules again, shall we?"

"Don't speak unless spoken to, don't make eye contact, don't flirt, don't ask questions," Thomas drawled. He almost seemed bored. "Oh, and don't bleed out and die."

My stomach clenched.

Heather did not seem amused. Her lips tightened before speaking. "Thank you, Thomas."

A bell sounded and Heather jumped to attention. "That would be our cue," she said. "Come with me."

Heather led us to the ballroom with the other group of Bloodletters not far behind us. We came to the ballroom well before any guests, which I was glad to be spared the embarrassment of being herded out in front of a crowd.

Waiters and waitresses stood with refreshments at the ready eyed us as we took our places as Heather showed us around the room. I avoided their disapproving stares, wondering as commoners who also toiled for the Royals, why they seemed to despise us.

A chamber orchestra was tuning and readying their instruments for the long night ahead. I watched them out of the corner of my eye for a while and then focused my attention on my silk gloves. Heather had laced my corset as tight as Greta's so I could only take shallow breaths.

In no time at all, the Royals began to trickle in. They were dressed in their finest clothing, darker shades of red, black and orange with gold trim. The ladies wore gowns with elaborate details and long trains, while the men were more reserved in tailored suits. They wore no masks, but I could not recognize any of them from my Sampling.

I stood at attention, resisting the urge not to sway to the beat of the waltz that the orchestra was playing. It knitted my fingers together and held my hands at my waist. I was grateful for the mask; its shadow allowed me to study the Royals as they socialized and danced.

I attended many balls in Wythtir. I was used to being in the center of the ballroom with a dance card in hand and sons of Councilors in waiting. This was a harsh contrast, standing near the wall as still as a statue, here for nothing but to satisfy the hunger of the Royals.

This ball was not unlike the ones I had attended, aside from being much more lavish. The ballroom was lit by golden chandeliers. The dark marble floor was polished to a mirror shine. The vaulted ceiling was painted with frescos depicting Gods of legend and the tall narrow windows gave a view of the expanse of gardens beyond.

There was a pause, and the song changed to a slower one. Some couples broke off for refreshments.

My heart fluttered nervously. Would any of them come for blood? So far tonight the Royals had been favoring the champagne. I lowered my eyes to the floor. We had been prepped, with Heather's help, before the ball with a butterfly needle and tube. A small clamp prevented any leaks. I hid the contraption up my glove. The needle bit at my skin when I moved, though she had tied it in place perfectly.

The ballroom was full now. Royals danced, talked, laughed and nibbled caviar on cucumber slices. A fleeting sadness filled my heart as I watched them, thinking of the life that my father had stolen away from me in a single night. I clenched my teeth and banished the memories for now.

"Excuse me, miss?"

A voice came to my ears, and I looked up from the polished floor. My heart stuck in my throat, but I managed to hold in a gasp as came face to face with the Baron. I bit down on my tongue in surprise; it was a miracle I did not show a hint of panic. "Yes, my Lord?" I tried to disguise my voice with an accent from the Northern provinces, the only one I had been ever good at mimicking.

The Baron smiled. I couldn't believe that I once found his face handsome. His hair was slicked back as usual. "I was wondering if you could spare me a taste, young lady."

My breath hitched. Did he know who I was? If I gave him blood, he would know without a doubt. Royals had such an excellent sense of taste. I suppressed a shudder.

"Well?" Lord Ramsey's tone grew impatient.

I smiled and bowed my head. "Of course, it would be my pleasure." I glanced around but Heather was nowhere in sight. I rolled down my long glove to reveal the needle and tubing. Lord Ramsey, knowing the process well, presented me with a tiny glass to fill. It was the same sort of glass that was used at my Sampling, barely a sip.

I filled the glass and pulled the glove up quickly. My mouth had gone dry with fear. If Lord Ramsey knew who I was, I had no doubt he would do something terrible. After Madam had sent him away last month, he would have had plenty of time to plot revenge against me.

All of my hopes were killed when I saw the familiar flame in his eye. He grinned and leaned close to me. "I knew it was you." He seized my arm and pulled me against him. "You little minx, thinking you could get away from me."

I gasped and turned my head. "Please, my Lord, not here," I whispered, barely loud enough to be heard over the music. "Madam was quite clear with you." I pulled my hand free.

Lord Ramsey glared at me. "Who do you think you are, girl?" He hissed and grabbed me again. "You're a Bloodletter. I take what I want from you."

I flinched as spittle landed on my cheek.

"Ah, Lord Ramsey," a man's voice came between us.

The Baron stepped back and turned to shake the man's hand. He was young, closer to my age than the Baron's. He was a Royal, dressed entirely in black with a red pocket square poking out of his jacket.

My breath hitched again, but for a very different reason. He was strikingly handsome. More than any man I had met in all my life. His pale blond hair was slicked back in the fashionable style, his eyes were a brilliant emerald green and he was tall enough that I had to tip my head to meet his gaze.

The man smiled apologetically. "Forgive us, Miss, but the Baron and I had something to discuss."

I bowed my head wordlessly as they walked away. I peeked up to see the Baron scowling in my direction. I breathed a sigh of relief and discretely leaned against the wall.

The orchestra played beautifully and never seemed to tire. As the night went on new Royals entered and some began to take their leave. I was only asked for blood from two other guests, both of whom I had never met before.

It was late in the evening when I was approached again. My face flushed when I saw the same young man who had saved me from the Baron. "Good evening, sir." I bowed my head.

"Evening Miss," the man replied. "How are you enjoying the evening?"

I bit my lip, knowing the rules about an unnecessary conversation with the Royals. "Very much, thank you."

The man smiled. "I hope that Lord Ramsey did not offend you," He spoke in a low voice close to my ear. "I have heard rumors of how he treats lovely Bloodletters like yourself and I felt the need to intercept him."

My face flushed. He was so close to me I could feel the warmth radiating off his skin. "I am grateful, thank you."

He smiled and stepped back. "You don't know who I am, do you?"

I hesitated, trying to match his features to any of the Royals I had met. "Apologies, but I do not."

The man chuckled. "You're new then."

I nodded.

"Do you mind if I get a taste?"

I nearly fainted. My hands were sweating inside my gloves. "Of course, my Lord." I fumbled as I pulled down my glove and unclipped the clamp on the end of the short tube. My blood filled the tiny glass, and I handed it back to the man.

He held it up to the light and inspected it like the Royals had done at the Sampling.

My mouth was dry, wondering what he would say. I surprised myself, actually wanting his approval of something that I had entirely no control over. I pinched myself and snapped out of it.

"Lovely," he said after draining the cup. He set it on a passing waiter's tray.

I wondered if my face was as red as it felt.

"May I ask, which House do you belong to?"

"I can't tell you," I sputtered, and the corrected myself. "I was told not to give out that information, the host's request, you see."

"Hm," He looked let down. "Very well." He took a step back from me.

My heart withered with disappointment.

"Then, may I know your name?"

I hesitated. As far as I had been told, that wasn't against any rules. "Violet." I whispered.

He grinned. "I guess your mother didn't name you for your hair then?"

I forced a laugh; unfortunately for him I had heard that joke a million times. "No, sir." It was very hard to flirt with a mask on, but I did my best to flutter my eyelashes.

He took my hand and kissed it. "Well, until the next event then, Miss." He turned and left, taking a piece of my heart with him.

FIFTEEN

"Do you have any idea who you were talking to?" Greta hissed through her teeth.

I looked out the window of the carriage we were sharing with Thomas and Heather. Thomas was asleep and Heather had decided to ride upfront with the coachman and get some air.

"No?" I asked incredulously. I had spoken to so many people in the six hours we were at the ball. My feet ached and all I could think about was a hot bath. Well, that and the mysterious blond stranger.

"No?" Greta squealed.

"Well, there was lots of guests, which one do you mean?"

Greta's mouth hung open in disbelief. She breathed in deeply to calm herself before continuing. "The Prince, Violet. Prince Isaac Saxon, second in line for the throne of Inwaed. Dear Gods, do you not know anything?"

Her insult passed over me in my shock. "The Prince?" I repeated.

Greta rolled her eyes. "Too bad his brother wasn't there, the Crown Prince, but I mean – he drank your blood, Violet! The Prince!" Thomas snorted in his sleep and Greta lowered her voice. "The Prince. I would kill for a chance like that."

Somehow, I didn't doubt she would. She rambled on, but I didn't hear a single word she said. The Prince. Prince Isaac. I had heard his name before many times, but I realized then that I had never seen a single photograph of him. I remembered my father saying that the Saxons liked to keep out of the spotlight as often as possible and that the King only intercepted politics when absolutely necessary. The Saxons, to me anyway, were names from textbooks. Distant and only slightly more tangible than characters from books.

The Prince had drank my blood, and he knew my name. I felt as giddy as a schoolgirl with a new crush. I stamped down on the emotion with all my might.

Greta voiced my internal thoughts. "Don't get your hopes up. It's not like he'll remember a lowly Bloodletter like you."

∞

I didn't tell a soul about my meeting with the Prince and I tried to keep my hopes down. Greta's excitement quickly turned to jealousy and she stopped talking to me again, not that I minded. The memory burned like a hot coal in my chest that I carried with me and used to warm myself whenever the dullness of the passing days became too much to bear.

As winter began to settle in, a bleak feeling began to fill the House. The clients became coming more often and we more demanding. When Heather took me to see Dr. Coleman because of my exhaustion he quickly dismissed it and cleared me for Bloodletting. I was beginning to wonder whose side he was on or if he switched whenever it suited him.

The feeling reached a climax when Thomas announced at lunch that Jack, his roommate, was not doing well. He was very weak and had been put on bedrest by the doctor.

My heart twisted at the thought of the thin, pale boy lying in bed alone.

"It's always this time of year." Penelope whispered. She set her fork down and left the table.

Thomas, who should have been the most distraught, set his jaw with determination. "He'll be fine. We've gone through this a few times," He insisted.

Amelia offered a weak smile. "I'm sure he will." Her uncertainty drifted around the room and we finished the meal in silence.

The news came only three days later – Jack had passed away in his sleep. Heather was the one to break it to us, but Thomas had been the one to discover it.

Heather sighed and crossed her arms, each hand gripping the opposite arm tightly. "He knew the risks," she said as if that would make us feel better.

I knew Jack had been here by his own freewill and my eyes slid to Amelia, who was hiding her face with her hands.

∞

Jack's death froze the inhabitants of the House in despair. Miss Prescott accidentally set a place setting at his chair four nights in a row before she broke the habit. Thomas was not his usual cheerful self, but cold and distant. Jack's death brought back Amelia's memories of Rose, and she retreated into herself. Greta, as usual, was the only one who acted normal at all and I wished she hadn't.

When I finally could not take the silence anymore, I decided to get out, if only for an hour. I dressed myself in a long black coat and scarf, wrapping the wool around my hair and neck. I crept out into the night. Everyone else was asleep.

The cold late November wind bit into my skin. I pushed my hands into the pockets of my coat and started walking.

I knew the area well enough by now, having gone out on errands with Heather and Greta enough times to recognize the streets even in the dark. The first snowfall of the season had fallen a few days ago, the frozen remains crunched under my boots.

I wandered around with no destination in mind. All I knew was that I needed to be away from the suffocating silence and sadness that had consumed the house. Hadn't everyone told me not to get attached? They had all said how short and unpredictable a Bloodletter's life was. Madam employed Jack for his own motives; none of us knew what they were, not even Thomas.

I pulled my scarf around my neck and blew warmth into my hands.

We would all move on just like the House had every other time. I hadn't even known Jack that well, but his death reminded me of my own mortality. We were all on the edge of death, just one slip away from a sickness or infection that would crush us into dust.

I looked up, suddenly not sure where I was. I had been following my feet mindlessly for a while now. I had passed the dress shop and the market. The buildings were empty and rundown on this side of town.

My mouth went dry, remembering the night that Heather had shown me the illegal Blood House. I turned on my heel and began following my footsteps back home.

I kept my eyes straight ahead and ignored the hair prickling at the back of my neck.

There were whispers. I blocked them out and quickened my pace.

Suddenly I ran into something dark and hard. I flew back, landing hard on the snowy cobblestones. I groaned. "Hey, watch where you're going." I looked up and locked eyes with a nameless Royal.

The Royal was older and dressed in tattered clothes. He had a wild expression. The man grinned at me, exposing yellowed teeth. "My, my," He said. "Don't you have beautiful red hair. I bet your blood is just as lovely."

A wave of nausea came over me. I scrambled to my feet. "Hardly," I tried to keep my composure. "Excuse me."

The man grabbed my coat as I tried to pass him. "I wasn't done with you, sweetheart."

A woman snickered behind me. "She's much too pretty to be in one of these Blood Houses. Which golden cage did you sneak out of?"

I shuddered, pulling away. "Let me go!"

The man seized my arm again and pulled me close to him. His breath reeked. "Not until we get a taste."

Suddenly, someone came between us and shoved him off. It was Victor, dressed in a warm cloak and wielding a kitchen knife.

"Violet!" Heather's voice was music to my ears.

I fell into her arms with a sob as she lectured me. I didn't even care that I upset her, I was just happy to be safe.

Victor brandished his knife. "Get lost!" He shouted.

The two Royals scurried off, not daring to fight the giant man.

Victor turned towards me. "You're lucky we found you! What were you thinking coming here in the middle of the night? This place is full of rogue Royals."

I gathered the strength I needed to stand on my own again. I didn't bother apologizing or asking why they followed me. Victor threw his cloak over my trembling shoulders and I was enveloped in sudden warmth. "Rogue?" I asked.

Heather shook her head, and the pair started guiding me home. "Violet, my dear child, there is so much about the Capital that you don't know."

SIXTEEN

DECEMBER BLEW IN WITH SOME OF THE WORST SNOWSTORMS I HAD EVER SEEN IN MY LIFE.

In Wythtir, the winters were generally short and mild, here in the Capital it was not uncommon to trudge through knee deep snow just to retrieve the mail.

I sat in my usual spot by the window in the parlor wasting the day away after all my clients had canceled because of the weather. I watched the blowing snow fly past the window, rattling the glass and howling like an invisible monster.

A gust of cold wind swept into the room as the front door opened and closed with a bang. Heather walked in while shaking snow from her hat and brushing off her long coat. She was clutching a bundle of mail in her hand. One envelope stood out, a jarring red amongst the shades of brown paper.

Heather saw me noticing the red letter and forced a smile. "Time for Collections."

"Already, but we just had one –"

"Six months ago," Heather interrupted me. "Yes, I know. That's how often they come." She stuck the mail under her arm and made her way to the kitchen. "Except they're less choosy in Winter, when their stock is starting to die off."

∞

"But Collections are usually after the Winter Festival?" Thomas asked in argument to Heather's announcement after dinner. He looked especially pale, his hair and skin had taken on a grayish tinge. In the weeks following Jack's death, his strength had been washed away until he was a shadow of his former self.

Heather shrugged and held up the bright red paper. "It seems that a flu has ripped through Brenhinyr and many of the Bloodletters have passed in their weakened state. There is a demand for Bloodletters who are already trained."

Brenhinyr was the most exclusive borough in the Capital. The ruling family lived there, along with the other nobility and politicians. The customers who came to Madam's Blood House in Afonyr were generally wealthy business owners, bankers, and the like.

While we paused in shock of the news of so many deaths, Greta's eyes lit up. "So, there are vacancies in the House of Strix?"

Heather surprised an annoyed sigh. "Yes, Greta."

Greta squealed. "Maybe this will be my chance," she said dreamily.

Thomas frowned. "Perhaps you missed the fact that over a dozen Bloodletters have died?"

Greta shrugged and pushed her dessert plate away. "Who cares? More for me."

The five of us gaped at her as she took her leave.

I looked down at my bread pudding and nudged it with the delicate silver dessert fork.

Amelia's hand shook as she attempted to bring a cup of tea to her mouth. She sighed and set it down with a clatter.

I hated to admit it to myself, but I found a small part of myself agreeing with Greta. Bloodletters died, it was the risk we took. Now maybe other deserving Bloodletters would go on to live posh, albeit short, lives. I knew that was what Greta wanted more than anything, at least she'd be out of our hair.

"One more thing," Heather added.

We looked up from our plates.

"It said in the letter that due to the shortage, every Bloodletter was required to give a sample for the Collection, even if they hadn't finished their one year waiting period," Heather bit the corner of her lip and looked at me. "So, Violet, that means you're eligible too."

∞

I laid awake that night while the rest of the House was asleep. I stared up at the ceiling, tossed and turned, braided my unruly hair, stretched, counted sheep and did about everything else I could think of before giving up on rest.

I quietly pushed my feet into my slippers and covered myself with my dressing gown. I went downstairs to the small library, finding my way without the help of any lights, save the moonlight that flowed through the windows.

I settled into a chair and cracked open a new book that Amelia had recommended. She knew all the best books in our library and had read them several times. This one was mostly poetry and even though I favored prose, I promised her I would give it a try. I smiled to myself, reading the titles. They were all romantic poems, silly verses of true love and soul mates.

I appreciated Amelia for her innocence and girlish ideals. I myself had given up on those naïve ideas of love a few years ago when my mother had told me that my father would no doubt be setting me up with one of the councilor's sons. Marriage was a business arrangement for people like us.

"Do you love Father?" I asked her.

My mother had smiled and kissed my forehead. "Yes, I do Violet," She said. "I love him very much.

But you'll realized that there is a difference between teenage crushes and matrimonial love. Young love burns hot and fast, as you grow older, you'll look for a love that runs slow and steady."

"Like molasses?"

My mother laughed until she cried.

I shook my head and rubbed my temples. It had been so long since I thought of her. Tears threatened to spill over before I clamped down on my emotions and brushed them away.

I heard a creak across the room. Rows of bookshelves separated the room into smaller sections. I set the book down and wove through the shelves to find the source of the sound. I was surprised to happen upon Greta, who was curled up asleep in a chair. I stepped back and my foot landed on a squeaky footboard.

Greta bolted upright, two thin books falling from her lap with a thump. "Who's there?" She gasped and locked eyes with me.

"Sorry, didn't mean to wake you," I stepped back again. "I didn't expect anyone else to be here at this time of night." I glanced down at the books that had fallen on the floor. They were small books with simple titles that looked to be written for young children.

Greta's face reddened enough to be seen in the dim lamplight. She kicked the books under the chair. "Never mind."

I cleared my throat. "Sorry," I apologized again without knowing why. "Were you reading those?"

"What's it to you?" She snapped. "Just because I'm an orphan you think I never learned to read?"

I was taken aback. "No!" I sprang to my own defense and then hesitated. "Wait, you're an orphan?"

Greta looked away and picked at the worn upholstery. "No one told you?"

"No one seems to gossip here except you," I sniffed.

Greta glared at me.

I sighed. "I honestly had no idea."

Greta crossed her arms. "Well, I am. That's why Madam took me in." She pulled her legs up to her chest. She suddenly looked small and vulnerable. Her hard facade was crumbling.

She didn't deserve my pity; I knew that, but found myself sitting down beside her anyways.

"I've been in this place for ten years. There's nothing else I know." Greta spoke into her arms. "Like I said before, this is all I'm good at." She laughed and shook her head. "That's why I have to be Collected, Violet. That's all that's left for me now."

I swallowed the lump in my throat. My heart felt for her, even if I didn't want it to. I hesitated before gently resting my hand on her shoulder. She flinched under my touch. "I won't say I understand, because I don't," I whispered. "But you know that that's no reason to be so cold to everyone."

Greta smirked and her mask slid into place. "Here's a tip, Violet. Don't get attached to anyone. Then it won't hurt when they leave."

∞

I carried Greta's warning with me the rest of the week. It weighed down on my chest like a stone. Her words made sense, and I realized that the next time I sat with them all. Thomas was withering away with grief. Penelope was as quiet as a mouse and Amelia was on edge every time someone referenced anyone who had passed. Greta was the only one who remained strong, with a hard indifference plastered on her face.

Doctor Coleman came to retrieve samples for the Collection. He seemed surprised to see me, but didn't say a word as he took my sample and filled out the paperwork. I heard him mumbling something about shortages as he left.

At night, Amelia was cursed with nightmares. Her screams woke me, her pleas not to be Collected.

I spent more and more time in the library; the only time I left was for meals and to meet clients. Unable to read the frivolous love poems, I immersed myself in history books. I slowly filled more gaps from my formal schooling.

As the week wore on, an odd feeling began to fill the House. It was like a morbid anticipation, like waiting for a guillotine to fall. On one side there was Amelia, who dreaded being Collected more than anything in the world and opposite her was Greta who prayed for it daily. Thomas and Penelope seemed neutral to the idea.

As for me, I wasn't sure how to feel. In less than a year, I would be a legal adult and be given the money set aside for me if I chose to leave. I often stared out the window, wondering where I would go or what I would do. Violet Ackerman, the old Violet, she was dead. I was in charge of my own destiny now and this newfound freedom was daunting.

"Aren't the results back yet?" Greta groaned in Heather's direction one day.

Amelia, Greta, and I were sitting in the parlor watching the snow fall. The Winter festival was only a week away.

Heather glared at Greta. "If they were, don't you think I would have told you?" She snapped. Our mentor was under severe stress. I had overheard her talking to Madam about getting more recruits in as soon as possible before our current customers lost interest with the lack of selection. I imagined it would be difficult to find young people willing to risk their lives on a daily basis to feed the Royals.

Greta glared back at Heather as she left.

"Don't be so hard on Heather." Amelia said.

Greta directed her fiery eyes to Amelia. "Excuse me?"

I held up my hands, trying to ease the tension in the room. "Please don't start, Greta."

"Me?" Greta snarled and pointed at Amelia. "She started it!"

Amelia hid her face behind her long brown hair.

"We're all waiting for the results, we all want them as bad as you do," I said.

Greta laughed. "You don't even know how bad I want them." She hissed.

"About as bad as I don't want them." Amelia mumbled.

Greta sneered in her direction and turned her attention to me. "What about you? Have you decided which you'd rather have?"

I hesitated. I was torn completely in two. "I don't know." I said finally.

Greta stood and leaned towards me, our noses nearly touching. "Well, let me tell you this. If you get Collected this time, you'd better hope they take you fast. Because if it's you over me," she barked out a bitter laugh. "I'll kill you before they get the chance to."

SEVENTEEN

I DID NOT TAKE GRETA'S THREAT LIGHTLY.

As the wait time stretched painfully, she became more worked up. She was like a rabid animal in a cage, pacing and snapping at anyone who dared speak to her.

I was finishing up an appointment with Lady Benedict when the news came. The Countess had taken her leave through the private exit for our patrons and I was applying a cold compress to a mark that I was sure would bruise when a cry rang out from downstairs.

The sound reminded me of a dying animal, high-pitched and strangled.

I flew to my feet, lifted my skirt, and ran down the stairs. I ran into the parlor and stopped to catch my breath.

Thomas, Greta and Amelia were together with Roger hovering nearby with a fistful of mail. Amelia was sitting with her hand on her forehead and staring at the ceiling. I knew that face; it was the same expression of relief that she wore last time they had passed her over. Thomas was reading a letter, his jaw set firmly. It was Greta who made the sound I heard. She was crying and jumping up and down in the middle of the parlor.

"Finally, finally, finally!" She giggled. Her face was glowing. She pressed her down letter to herself, crumpling the paper against her chest.

My mouth went dry. These mixed reactions could only mean that they had received the results of the Collection.

Heather came up behind me. "Ah, Violet, there you are. I was looking for you," she said.

Roger handed me an envelope and spoke to Heather. "And Miss Penelope?" He asked.

"Still in an appointment," Heather replied. "Here, I'll take her letter so you can get back to what you were doing."

Roger nodded, gave Heather the last envelope, and left.

Greta's cheers had fallen silent. She narrowed her eyes at me. "So? Aren't you going to open it?"

I stared at the envelope in my hand. It was marked with the official seal of Inwaed, with the House's address and my name written in black ink. My hands

169

trembled as I broke the red wax seal and pulled the letter free. I unfolded it slowly and licked my lips.

Dear Violet

C/O Mme G. Desjardins - Registered Blood House No. 53

We are pleased to inform you that you have been approved for a position as a private Bloodletter for the House of Strix, in accordance with the Bloodletting Regulation Act. Despite your brief service record, your blood has passed our highest of standards.

A brief training session will take place on January 1st, and upon satisfactory completion, you will be signed under a new contract with the House of Strix. Your current contractor has been contacted and informed of this change.

Congratulations on your acceptance.

I couldn't believe my eyes. I read the short letter repeatedly. It was straight and to the point yet left so many questions unanswered.

"Well, what does it say?" Greta's voice washed over Amelia's identical question.

I folded the letter carefully and took a deep breath before answering. "I've been accepted at the House of Strix."

∞

"So, the House of Strix," Amelia murmured. She had cried herself dry by now.

"Yeah," I said, staring at my hands. We were in our room and the house was quiet. The wind could be heard outside our window but at least the snow had stopped for now.

Amelia rolled over and propped herself up on her elbows. Her round blue eyes were bloodshot. "What's it like?"

"What's what like?"

"Being Collected."

I laughed. "I don't know. Can't really say yet." I folded and unfolded the letter again. It hadn't left my hands all evening.

"Are you excited?" Amelia asked.

I bit my lip. "No, not really," I replied. "I was just getting comfortable here and now it's all going to change."

"Well, at least you'll have Greta," Amelia said.

Greta had also been accepted to the House of Strix. I was not sure if that was a blessing or a curse. I made a face and my roommate laughed. "Yeah, great," I said sarcastically. "Oh well, it's only ten months until my birthday and then we'll see."

Amelia tipped her head to one side. "What do you mean?"

"Well, when I'm a legal adult. Then who knows what I'll be doing."

Amelia sucked in a breath. "Oh, right." She sat up and played with the edge of her quilt. "You don't know then." She trailed off.

I furrowed my brow. "Know what?"

Amelia blushed; the color was shocking against her pale face. "Oh, nothing, forget I said anything."

"Amelia," I groaned. "Please don't do this to me. You can't keep avoiding telling me things."

"It's Heather's job."

I sighed. "Amelia, please, you're my only true friend in this place. What don't I know?" I was sure that I could fill a book with what I didn't know about Bloodletting at this rate. I was getting tired of everyone thinking I couldn't handle information.

"Well, when someone is Collected, it's forever." Amelia broke her silence.

"What do you mean, forever?"

"Like, forever. Collections have different contracts. The only way out is to be given your freedom willingly, or, um,"

"Die?"

Amelia looked away. "Yeah," she breathed.

I sat dumbly for a moment before crushing the letter in my fist.

∞

The Winter Festival was a somber affair in the Blood House.

Victor tried his best to bring our spirits up by baking an assortment of cookies, pies, and other treats. We sat down to a lavish ham dinner and though it smelled wonderful, it tasted like ash in my mouth.

Greta hummed to herself happily as she ate. We ignored her.

172

"So, what house have they sent you to, Thomas?" I asked.

Thomas' grip tightened on his glass of wine. "Beaucourt." He said stiffly.

Greta's interest peeked. "Oh, that's very nice," she complimented. "Such an influential family."

Thomas silenced her with a look. "Yes, I would prefer that my killers be educated and well-traveled," he said sarcastically.

Amelia pushed the potatoes around her plate and sighed. "I'm going to miss you all."

My chest tightened for her, but at least she was still safe with Madam. Well, as safe as a Bloodletter could be. I glanced at Penelope, who would also be left behind, but her expression was unreadable. I hoped that once we were gone, she would open up to Amelia, so they wouldn't be totally alone.

Greta went back to humming under her breath and smiling.

Thomas stared at her incredulously and drained his glass of wine. "Well," he said. "It was nice knowing all of you." He gritted his teeth and stood.

Amelia gasped. "Don't say it like that, you make it sound like goodbye."

Thomas frowned. "Well, that's what it is, isn't it?" He ignored her protest and left without looking back.

∞

The week after the Winter Festival flew by in an instant.

All my client's appointments were canceled, save Lady Benedict, I had wanted to say goodbye to her personally, as she was the most respectful of all the Royals I had met thus far. She seemed shocked when I told her where I was off to, but she smiled and nodded. "Good luck, Violet." She kissed my forehead before leaving.

My last night in the house I pulled my suitcase out from under the bed and packed it with my few belongings. I left two of my dresses for Amelia, though they might be a size too big for her. At the bottom of my drawers I found the photograph of my mother and the front page of the newspaper that I had saved.

ACKERMAN FAMILY MOURNS DEATH OF HEIR.

That seemed like a lifetime ago, but I couldn't let them go yet. I folded them carefully and hid them in the inner pocket of my suitcase before snapping it shut.

Amelia came in without knocking and made a surprised sound.

I looked over my shoulder and smiled at her. "Hi."

"Hi," she mumbled and sank down onto her bed. There was a fresh bandage tied around her arm and her eyes were dark.

I watched her. She would have to survive two more years of this before she could leave and follow her dream. Surely by then she would have saved an excellent sum for a dowry and a fine-boned, pretty girl like her would have no shortage of suitors. I wondered, though, if anyone would want a bride who was once a Bloodletter. If they would question her morals. I let the questions slide away, not wanting to upset her on our last night together.

"When are you leaving?" Amelia asked.

I glanced at my suitcase. "Early tomorrow morning. Heather said a carriage will come for Greta and me." Thomas had already left yesterday and there was a hole in our dinner that could not be replaced.

Amelia shivered and moved closer to the radiators. She rubbed her arms.

I sat down beside her. "I'll write you."

Amelia nodded. "Please do, I'll be worrying sick about you."

"Don't worry about me," I said. "You need to worry about yourself. Don't give up on your dream and don't you dare die."

Amelia's blue eyes softened, and her lip trembled. "Promise me that you won't die, and I'll do the same."

I laughed and shook my head. "I'm already dead."

Amelia gasped. "Please don't say that!"

I paused, forgetting for a moment how sensitive she was. "I didn't mean it literally. Just the old me, the Violet that first walked through these doors. She's gone." I put my hands between my knees so she wouldn't notice them shaking.

Amelia nodded. "I know what you mean."

My heart fluttered. Since receiving my acceptance letter, there had been a faint feeling of excitement in my chest, even though being Collected was a death sentence. I bit my lip, wondering if I should share my feelings with Amelia. "Amelia, to be honest," I said slowly. "I'm kind of excited."

Amelia paled. "Excited? What kind of person are you?"

I shook my head. "It's hard to explain, but it's a new adventure. I've been thinking about it a lot lately. My mother used to say that everything happens for a reason, and to be honest, I always laughed behind her back about it." I swallowed, forcing my voice to stay steady. "But now, I think maybe she's right."

Amelia nodded.

"And," I continued before the words died in my throat. "Well, at the Autumn Festival ball, I met someone from the House of Strix. I think."

Amelia gasped and lean forward. "What? Why didn't you tell me?"

"I didn't think it was that important, a onetime thing," I said. "But I met the Prince, Prince Isaac."

Amelia squealed and slapped her hand over her mouth. "The Prince?" She hissed once she had control over her volume again.

I nodded. "So, I guess maybe I'm looking forward to seeing him again." I flushed. "Except he doesn't know who I am." Greta's words rang in my head. "He wouldn't care about a Bloodletter anyway."

Amelia reeled and clapped her hands. "He may not know your face, but he'd know your blood if he tasted it. Oh, it's like a fairy tale!"

Her enthusiasm embarrassed me. "I doubt I'll get assigned to him."

"Maybe not," she admitted. "But if it's meant to be."

I cut her off, not wanting to get ahead of myself. "I doubt it," I sighed and put a stop to the conversation.

The corners of Amelia's lips turned up in a tiny smile and she spoke in a sing-song voice. "Well, you just said it yourself, everything happens for a reason."

EIGHTEEN

THE HOUSE OF STRIX LEFT ME BREATHLESS.

I had seen photos and drawings in my textbooks and the newspapers, but nothing could have prepared me for the grandness of the palace. It stood four stories high. A low, wide set of marble stairs led up to the front door that was framed by pilasters. If looking form above, the palace would form a slightly curved shape and, behind it, acres of land contained within high stone walls.

Both Greta and I stared out the window as the carriage pulled up the private road that wove around snow-covered gardens. The heavy iron gates clanged shut behind us.

Greta was twitching with excitement. She was so overjoyed that I had been spared any icy, sarcastic remarks as we left the Blood House behind.

The coachman brought the pair of black horses to a stop and the footman opened the carriage door for us. Greta wrapped her cloak around herself tightly and took the footman's hand. He helped her out and then I followed.

I held in a gasp, keeping my expression indifferent and gazed up at the palace towering above us. The snow had been cleared from the walkway.

"This way, my ladies." The footman said as he guided us up the stairs and to the front door. He had barely spoken the entire trip, choosing to ride upfront with the coachman instead of inside with us. He was handsome, but when Greta fluttered her eyelashes at him, he ignored her.

Greta picked up her skirts and followed him up the stairs. She had worn her most expensive gown today, which took up more than her share of space inside the carriage. I had opted for something simpler and suited for traveling.

The massive front doors swung open and revealed a servant who inclined his head in a polite bow. As far as I could tell, all the servants I had seen so far were commoners and this did not surprise me. Simple tasks like cleaning, cooking, and driving were no doubt beneath the Royals.

Inside the vestibule, another nameless servant took our coats and bags from us with a bow.

"Welcome to the House of Strix, ladies," said the footman. "I will show you to the waiting room."

I was thankful for my upbringing, which blessed me with the ability to not end up like Greta, who was gaping like a fish. I smiled demurely and nodded.

The red carpet was plush, and the walls covered in paintings and portraits of all sizes. The coffered ceilings with golden inserts gleamed in the glow of the lights spaced evenly along the walls. Elaborate mahogany moldings framed each room we passed.

If the grandness of the front hall was any indication of the rest of the palace, I decided it would be a very lovely place to die.

We followed the footman down a maze of hallways until we reached a small sitting room. A maid was there laying out a tea and sandwiches. She left with a silent bow.

It was only then that I realized I was starving. I had no appetite for breakfast before we left. Only Heather had been there to see us off, and I was glad that I wouldn't have to face Amelia one last time. I hated goodbyes.

"Please rest here, ladies," the footman instructed. "I'm sure you will find it comfortable. In the meantime, Lady Carrol is expecting you and shall meet you shortly."

I nodded. "Thank you, sir." I glanced at Greta, but she was absorbed in the surrounding finery.

The footman smiled and shut the door. A click indicated that he had locked us in.

I frowned. Locked into another room, this was becoming all too familiar. My stomach rumbled, so I sat and helped myself to tea. The sandwiches were made with paper-thin slices of bread and strawberry jam.

Greta roamed around the room, looking at the paintings that hung on the walls. She hummed to herself, the same jaunty tune that she had sang since being Collected. The blond looked over her shoulder at me. "Really, Violet, how can you be stuffing your face at a time like this?"

"I hardly consider two bites to be stuffing myself," I shot back and sipped the tea.

Greta sniffed and settled on the sofa across from me. She pulled a small hand mirror from a pocket in the depths of her large pleated skirt and checked her hair. She closed the tiny mirror with a snap that echoed in the silence.

"Greta," I said, remembering something that had bothered me since the day we received our letters. "How did you know that you were accepted?" I hesitated when she raised her eyebrows at me. "That is, how did you read your letter?"

Greta's cheeks blazed red. "I can read, thank you very much," she snapped. "Maybe not enough to do it for pleasure, but I'm not an idiot!"

I had expected her to react that way. "Sorry, just curious." I looked back down at my tea.

Lady Carrol made her entrance a while later. She was a short, plump woman with rosy cheeks and dark hair piled high on her head. "Good morning, ladies," she said. Her purple taffeta gown swished and crinkled as she moved. "I take it you are the new recruits that Madam Desjardins has sent?"

Greta and I both flew to our feet and nodded.

"Right," Lady Carrol said and clasped her hands behind her back. Her opal earrings glinted in the light. She wasted no time, scurrying around us and inspecting us from head to toe, muttering under her breath. She flipped down a pair of glasses that had been nestled in her hair to inspect the tiny scars that dotted the inside of our arms. Without ceremony, she produced syringes and took a small sample from each of us.

When she was satisfied, she took a step back. "I've reviewed the files that Dr. Coleman had sent ahead, and everything seems to match up," Lady Carrol said with a smile. "Welcome to the House of Strix."

∞

After Lady Carrol was done with us, we were sent to our private quarters.

I was surprised to find out that I would not be sharing a room with Greta; I sent a thankful prayer skywards. My room was small by Royal standards. Though it was lovely for a room befitting a servant. It was tastefully decorated, with a large bed, table, wardrobe and vanity.

The Bloodletters were kept in a wing on the east side of the house. Our quarters were not in the basement, like the other servants. The Saxon family took up residence in private apartments on the top floor of the palace. Between us were hundreds of rooms for guests, meetings, and parties.

I was happy to have a room at the end of the hall. Greta's room was across from mine. Lady Carrol, who was the caretaker of the Bloodletters, had a room at the opposite end of the hall. One had to walk past her room to go anywhere but the washroom. She was like some obscure nanny, I thought.

I flung myself onto the bed and wrapped myself in the warm red blankets. My body sank into the softness of the mattress and within minutes, my mind surrendered to sleep.

I dreamed of the Blood House. Madam, Amelia, Heather, Vincent, and quiet Miss Prescott. The Baron infiltrated my sleep for the first time in days, his hungry eyes and wicked tongue lashed out at me. I dreamed of the Blood House in the slums, the rotting body of a cast off Bloodletter left in the streets. The

Royals with eyes like wild animals and the Royals who treated me like a precious flower.

I woke gasping and sweaty. There was a knock at my door.

"Dinner, Miss." A voice passed through the crack under the heavy door.

I flew from my bed and opened the door.

A maid was carrying a covered food tray. A cart filled with identical trays was parked behind her. She walked around me with short quick steps and set the tray down on the table. "I hope everything is to your liking." She bowed and continued down the hall.

I opened my mouth to call after her, but she was already knocking at Greta's door. I shut mine quickly and turned the lock with a sigh. I wondered if there would be communal meals with the other Bloodletters, or if I would sit waiting in this room until a Royal fancied himself a taste.

With a sigh, I sat down at the table and lifted the silver cover from the plate. The generous portion of beef stew and biscuits smelled wonderful, but I looked away and slammed the cover down again. I looked out the window and muttered. "What have we gotten ourselves into, Violet?"

NINETEEN

"AND ONE AND TWO AND THREE, OH! PAY ATTENTION, GRETA!" Lady Carrol shrieked. She slammed her hands down on the piano keys and stood, her fists planted on her wide hips.

Greta laughed nervously. "Sorry, ma'am."

We were in the music room. Lady Carrol was doing her best to teach Greta a simple court dance that I had learned as a child.

Bloodletters in the House of Strix were expected to do much more than stand and give blood, as I had found out. This past week we had been woken and dawn for rigorous lessons on etiquette, dance, and music. While Greta had thrived with the piano, she danced like a drunken dog.

185

I stifled a laugh from where I sat. Lady Carrol had known that I was a Bloodletter from a well-to-do family and she had been impressed with me thus far, but I would not take any chances. My musical skills were rudimentary at best.

Greta glared at me and adjusted her voluminous green dress. Yesterday we had been fitted for new gowns, but for now we were wearing whatever the deceased Bloodletters had worn before us. My stomach twisted just thinking about it.

Every morning before our lessons, a maid came to my room, dressed me, applied makeup and pinned my hair. She was unexperienced with curls and brushed my hair to an unidentifiable frizz until I managed to convince her I was competent enough with the fashionable styles.

Lady Carrol pinched the bridge of her nose, as I had seen her do countless times before when she was frustrated. She cleared her throat and motioned to me. "Violet, could you please step in?"

I nodded and went to Greta's side. I took her hand and tried my best to lead her through the simple dance steps and the Lady started the song over.

Greta's face pinched. "Show off." She hissed under her breath.

"I can't help it, you know," I whispered back and suppressed a yelp as she stepped on my foot.

Greta's eyes grew round. "Oops, I'm sorry. I can't help it, you know."

I gritted my teeth. "You know, when I found out we were coming to Strix together, part of me hoped that maybe we could put aside our differences and be friends."

Greta scowled.

"If not friends, at least civil with each other?" I tried. She stumbled again, and I kept us on pace. "At least for the training?"

Greta's mouth twitched as she considered what I was saying. "Let's just get through this."

The piano music came to an end. "Much better, girls!" Lady Carrol beamed.

I let Greta's hand fall and stepped away to nurse my throbbing toes.

Aside from training, we were kept confined to our rooms. I was eager to meet the other Bloodletters, who, based on the number of doors, there were ten of us. One day during a break from our etiquette lessons on addressing different members of nobility, I mentioned this to Lady Carrol.

"Excuse me, my Lady?"

Lady Carrol smiled. "Ma'am is fine for me, dear," she said. "But I'm happy that you were paying attention."

Greta huffed and rolled her eyes.

I ignored her. "Yes, Ma'am. I was wondering when we would meet the other Bloodletters?"

Lady Carrol stared at me steadily before replying. "Why is that?"

I suddenly felt nervous. "Well, with Madam Desjardins, we ate and enjoyed each other's company during our off times."

Lady Carrol chuckled. "I see, well, you are a Bloodletter for the House of Strix now. You're never off duty." She looked at me pointedly and then to Greta.

I swallowed.

"Though, I'm sure you'll meet the other girls, eventually."

"Girls?" Greta exclaimed. "You mean, there are no male Bloodletters?"

Lady Carrol shook her head. "Of course, there are but we keep them in a separate wing from you girls." She paused. "I assume that you both came from a co-ed Blood House?"

We nodded in unison.

Lady Carrol seemed just the slightest bit scandalized. "Well, there won't be any of that here. Leads to complications, you see." She sipped her water.

I didn't need to think hard to know what those complications might be.

∞

After dinner, and with Lady Carrol's permission, I returned to the music room to practice with the piano. I let the ticking of the metronome guide me through the simple songs but fumbled as soon as I had to use both hands in unison. I sighed and rested my forehead on the piano with a clunk of white and black keys.

"Having trouble?"

I swung myself upright and glared at Greta. She was holding a book of poetry in her hand. "No," I said firmly and turned my attention back to the sheet music.

Greta sat beside me on the bench without invitation. She looked at the notes. "You'll really have to stretch your hands to play that piece." She demonstrated and tapped the keys. "See?"

I tried to stretch my pinky finger to reach the black key and missed. I sighed.

"You'll get it," she said. "I've been playing for years."

I cracked my knuckles and tried again without success. "You said you were poor; how did you learn?"

"Teresa taught me."

I looked at her questioningly.

"Teresa was our mentor before Heather," Greta explained. "She retired during my second year there. But, before she did, she taught me how to play on the quiet days." She set left hand on the keys and played a scale perfectly.

I nodded. I could never imagine anyone else mentoring the House except Heather. She was such a perfectionist, so passionate and dutiful. With a shiver, I remembered the night she spoke to me frankly, thinking I was drugged beyond memory. *I've given my blood to them for twenty years. They can give me some of theirs.*

"So," Greta continued. "I was thinking." She lifted the poetry book from her lap. "Lady Carrol is starting poetry lessons tomorrow." She chewed her bottom lip, her cheeks turning red.

I looked at the book; it was a book full of classics older than the Royals. "You can't read them, can you?"

Greta shook her head. Her long fair fell over her face. "No," she mumbled. "It's too complicated."

I took the book from her hand and grimaced. "She couldn't pick something more modern?" I sighed and opened the first bookmarked page. "Death Be Not Proud."

Greta shivered. "Such lovely subject matter."

We spent the better part of the next hour going over the first poem line by line. By the end of it, I wasn't sure if she was reading or had just memorized it, but it would keep Lady Carrol happy for now. When we both could not possibly read another word, I handed her back the book, and we went our separate ways.

∞

Any warmth that I may have felt towards Greta vanished the next day. The dresses that had been ordered for us came in and while I was awestruck with the bold tones and intricate details, Greta only found flaws.

I sat on the sofa watching her try them on. I felt like a doll sitting in the layers of silk. It was the perfect shade of blue that complimented both my eyes and my amber hair at the same time. It had a low square neckline and cap sleeves. The unique weave shimmered in the light.

Greta pouted, fidgeting with the lace overlay on a black evening gown. "It's just not right."

"First the beige one was too light, now that one is too dark. For goodness sakes, Greta, it's black!" I said, exasperated.

She looked in the mirror and glared at my reflection. The seamstress was busy at her feet, altering the hem that was, in Greta's opinion, too long. "This is why I wanted them to order my dresses from Maurice."

The seamstress tutted, pulling a pin from her mouth. "Maurice is a common tailor. The House of Strix employs only the best designers."

Greta made a shrill sound in her throat and stomped her foot down on the stool she stood on. "How dare you!"

I rolled my eyes and snuck away from the bickering pair. All this dress talk was making me sick. I slipped into the hallway and turned the corner. I walked quickly and quietly, hoping no one would catch me on my way to the library, where we had studied poetry that morning.

The wide mahogany doors greeted me. I pulled the handle and creeped inside. The smell of dust and paper greeted me like an old friend. While the library in the Blood House had been small, cramped, but adequate, this library was as grand as the rest of the palace. It was two stories high, with tall shelves running up every wall. A metal spiral staircase led up to the upper level, where sofas and chairs in every corner.

I peered around and listened for the telltale sounds of turning pages. When I was sure I was alone, I ran up the stairs, plucked the first book that I came to off the shelf and nestled into a chair. From where I was sitting, I could see the door in case anyone came looking for me, but if I ducked down, they would likely have a hard time seeing me.

Once we were done with fittings, Greta and I were instructed to return to our rooms for dinner, surely the maid wouldn't think twice if I wasn't there.

I opened the book, happy to find that it was an anthology of more modern poetry. Reading the classics, although they were necessary for any well brought up lady, were exhausting and dry. Poetry had grown on me during the time I spent reading with Amelia.

Several pages later, I heard a creak as the door opened. I held my breath and sunk into the leather armchair.

A young man walked in. He was tall and lean with blond hair so light it nearly blended into his pale skin. His face was angular and dreadfully handsome. I recognized him immediately as the Royal who I had met at the party.

Prince Isaac.

I sank back further.

The Prince's shoes clicked against the hardwood floor, echoing in the room's silence. By the sound of his steps, he was pacing through the shelves on the lower level.

I held my breath. There was only one exit and he would no doubt see me if I tried to make a run for it. I held the poetry book to my chest and quickly retreated to a chair at the very back of the upper level, hidden behind tall bookcases covered in dust and weighed down by heavy encyclopedias.

There was a creak of springs. The Prince must have sat down on a sofa. Aside from the occasional sound of paper, the room was silent again.

I bit my lip. I was trapped now until he decided to leave and who knew how long that would be. I assumed that a prince would have a lot of free time on his hands to do whatever he pleased. Then my nose began to tickle. I clamped my hand over my face, cursing the dusty books. I felt a sneeze coming on. I counted backwards from twenty, pinching my nose and waiting for the feeling to pass. Then, just as I was letting my guard down, I sneezed. It was a loud, unladylike sound that broke through the silence like a gunshot.

"Hello?" The furniture creaked. "Is someone there?"

My heart fluttered at the sound of his voice before I got a grip on myself and realized my dilemma.

Footsteps again. The clicking echoed as he walked up the metal stairs. "Hello? Show yourself!" His voice switched from curious to authoritative.

I sank back in the chair and hugged my knees to my chest, seeing his shadow on the ceiling. The library was large, but not big enough that it would take him long to find me stowed away in the dark forgotten corner of outdated tomes.

As his footsteps grew closer, I made a snap decision. Clutching the book, I emerged from the safety of the bookcases and came face to face with the Prince. "Your Majesty!" I feigned surprise.

The Prince took a step back. He looked startled for only an instant. "Oh, thank goodness. I thought maybe you were an assassin out to kill me."

My sharp wit won over my etiquette training. "Maybe I am, you'd never suspect." I looked down quickly, tightening my fists in frustration.

Prince Isaac laughed. "Well, if they do send an assassin, I would pray that she has as lovely face as yours to be my last memory."

My cheeks burned. "I apologize, Your Majesty."

"Not at all." The Prince reached out slowly and touched my cheek. He paused, his brow furrowing. "You seem very familiar." He laughed and shook his head. "But surely I would remember the name of such a beautiful young woman."

I flushed, my hands wringing a layer of my blue skirt. "And I would have remembered meeting you, Your Majesty." I bowed my head again.

"Are you one of the new Bloodletters, then?" The Prince asked.

"Yes, sir."

The Prince smiled. It was a genuine smile that was full of light. "Welcome to the House of Strix," he said. Somehow, when it was coming from him, it didn't sound so ominous.

I was melting in the heat of his emerald eyes. Remembering the legends, I had read in my previous life, I always imagined that Royals would be like him. My awe had been diluted in the time I had spent in the Capital. Very few Royals had such a powerful presence.

"Well, I should be getting back," I said, setting the book of poetry back in its place.

"Alright," Prince Isaac said, shoving his hands in his pockets and looking more like an ordinary boy than a demigod. "You can borrow that if you want." He nodded towards the book.

I brushed my fingertips down the leather spine and pulled it from the shelf again. "Thank you." I bowed low and dashed down the stairs. I didn't look back, but I could feel his gaze burning into my skin.

TWENTY

I WAS AWAKE HALF OF THE NIGHT SITTING IN BED AND READING THE BOOK. I finished it the day after, just so I would have a reasonable excuse to go back to the library.

Thinking back, I had never been smitten by any of the potential suitors that I had been introduced to. Sure, there was a few that piqued my interest and even less that I exchanged heated kisses within hidden places, but none had made my heart burst like the Prince.

I knew that I was being ridiculous, no Prince would ever be interested in a Bloodletter like me. Even before all this mess, as a Minister's daughter, I wouldn't have stood a chance. Royals never socialized with outsiders, except for business or politics.

After lunch I snuck out of my room to bring the book back to the library. I was passing Lady Carrol's door when it swung open.

"Ah, Violet, perfect timing. I was just going to call for you."

I stopped mid-step and swerved to face her.

The Lady glanced down at the book in my hand. "And just where were you going with that?"

"Uh," I fumbled and held the book to my chest. "Oh, well you see I grabbed it during our last lesson so I could brush up on my reading. You see, before I was so busy with Bloodletting, I didn't get much time for reading and I've missed several new poets. I was just going to bring it back –"

Lady Carrol held up her hand to silence me. "Never mind," She sighed and held out her hand. I gave her the book and she continued. "I appreciate a well-read young lady, but you know Bloodletters are not allowed to be roaming the halls." She tucked the book under her arm. "I'll have a maid bring this back for you."

I nodded. "Yes Ma'am."

Lady Carrol gestured to her room. "Please, come inside. I want to talk to you."

My heart pounded. Had she been told about my run in with the Prince? Had he complained that Bloodletters were running wild through the palace? I didn't think he'd be the kind of person to do that sort of thing, but if I were honest with myself, I didn't even know him.

Lady Carrol's room was divided into a large office and private bedroom. The wallpaper was pink with a while floral design that matched the curtains. She set the book on her desk and sat down. "You've impressed me, thus far, Violet."

I sat down across from her, tucking my skirt under myself carefully. "Thank you."

The Royal smiled. "When I read your profile, I was most intrigued. I spoke to Madam Desjardins personally and you came highly recommended. It's not often that we encounter Bloodletters with good breeding."

I tried not to grimace at that description, making me feel like a pet rather than a person.

"As you can imagine, most of our stock comes from poorer families," Lady Carrol continued. The gold ring on her finger flashed in the light. "Madam Desjardins refused to give me your family name as was stated on your contract, but that is no matter to me. I would like to make sure that your talents and delicious blood are put to good use."

I suppressed a cringe. So, there was a taste test after all.

"So, after speaking with my superiors, it has been decided that you will be assigned to His Majesty Prince Edmund."

My heart jumped at the word Prince before it was squashed with the name. "Prince Edmund?"

Lady Carrol grinned. "Yes, I know, this must be exciting for you. A personal Bloodletter to the Crown Prince! But it is necessary, as personal Bloodletters are very visible in the public eye and our future king deserves only the best."

I managed a weak smile. "Oh, I see."

"Speechless?" She laughed. "Oh child, this is a great honor. I'm so proud of you."

"Yes," I said softly. "What about Greta?"

The Lady's smile drooped. "Oh, that girl," She sighed. "She'll find a place soon enough." She clapped her hands together. "Never mind about her, there's work to be done. The Saxon's personal Bloodletters are kept close to their apartments, you won't need to worry about being cooped up in here anymore. Oh and you'll need more dresses!"

"Great…" I tried to sound enthusiastic, but my voice fell flat.

∞

The staff wasted no time in moving me into a new room. While they bussed my ever-expanding wardrobe across the palace, I hovered around Greta's door, waiting for her to come out. I raised my hand to knock several times but lost the courage and let my hand fall back down.

Greta was a wild one, unpredictable and untrustworthy in my eyes. I pitied her more than cared for her. If I told her that I had been chosen to be a Bloodletter for Prince Edmund, I had no doubt that it would only infuriate her. I brushed my hand along the doorframe and turned away.

The Saxon's private apartments were on the west side of the palace and I was pleased to find that they were closer to the library than the other Bloodletters' rooms had been.

This room was decorated with bold colors and dark wooden furniture. A large four-poster bed, a wardrobe, a desk and a small round table and chairs. A pair of glass doors let in light from outside, leading to balconette that overlooked the snowy palace grounds. The top floor offered an unobstructed view of the world beyond. A door was ajar, and I was surprised to see that it led to a modest bathroom. Even in my days growing up in the manor, I had never had my own private bathroom.

Lady Carrol caught the gleam in my eye that I hadn't hidden in time. "Lovely, isn't it, my dear?" She clasped her hands behind her back, watching the pair of servants organizing my clothing.

I nodded, not trusting myself to speak.

"Just remember, the position of a personal Bloodletter is as wonderful as it is precarious," Lady Carrol warned. Her voice was low and steady. "Win the Prince's favor, or be cast away like a broken toy, that is up to you."

∞

I carried the weight of her warning to me closely.

Once I was left alone, I washed, groomed and dressed myself. I picked a flowing blue gown with laces at the sides. I cinched myself in, but unlike the servants who had been dressing me recently, made sure to leave some space to breathe. I pulled my damp amber curls into a loose bun at the base of my neck. On top of the wardrobe was a small jewelry box filled with earrings and necklaces. I added a set of pearl earrings to my ensemble.

I looked myself up and down in the long mirror that stood beside my wardrobe. I smoothed down the airy silk that hung in layers at my hips. I was impressed with myself, looking more like a grown woman every day. The weeks free of Bloodletting had brought the feminine curves back to my body and the glow back into my cheeks.

The Prince ought to be impressed.

I wandered over to the window and looked out to the snowy grounds that stretched beneath me. Groundkeepers were clearing the freshly fallen snow from the walkways that wove through the sleeping gardens like a spider's web. The move had taken nearly all afternoon, and the sun was beginning to set.

My stomach grumbled a warning that dinnertime would be any minute now. As if on cue, there was a brisk knock at my door and a maid entered with a tray of food. Whatever it was, it smelled delicious, but my hopes of having social meals were squashed again.

The maid set the tray down on the table. "Dinnertime, Miss," she said. She kept her eyes on the ground when speaking to me.

"Thank you," I replied. Noticing the same tense feeling radiating from her as all the other servants I had encountered. "Excuse me, but could I know your name?"

The maid shook her head. "No, Miss, please don't. We're not supposed to be familiar with the Bloodletters." She whispered. She had a Northern accent.

I raised my eyebrows. "Why ever not?"

The maid's face paled and her hands shook as she placed the silverware on the table. "Not my place, miss." She wilted under the determined glare I sent at her. "It's just that, you're all short lived, miss. Don't need to be getting attached." She scurried out without another word.

My stomach sank. Suddenly I didn't feel so hungry.

∞

As Lady Carrol had predicted, the Prince did not come to meet me until late in the evening. They had left me alone with my thoughts and a cold plate of dinner for hours.

Just as I was thinking about getting changed for bed, there was a very soft knock at the door.

I bolted up from my seat and smoothed the wrinkles out of my dress. I took a quick glance at the mirror to check my hair before calling out. "Come in, please."

The door opened and a young man entered. He was, if I had to guess, only a few years older than Prince Isaac, but he could have not looked more different. He was slightly shorter, with a boyish face, big dark eyes and black hair cut into a short, military style. He wore a crisp white shirt and matching gray trousers and vest. His gold cufflinks glinted in the light.

I bowed my head low. "Your Majesty," I greeted.

Prince Edmund said nothing, his hands falling to his sides and no expression crossing his pale face as he looked me up and down. "Hm, so you're the new Bloodletter that Lady Carrol has sent me?"

I nodded. I had grown tense under his indifference. I bit the side of my cheek and smiled. I had worked for hours to be a picture of elegance and he hadn't even seemed the least bit impressed.

"Alright," the Prince sighed. "I guess you'll do."

I flushed furiously, biting into my cheek until I tasted blood.

Prince Edmund took a step forward, tapping his chin. He walked around me twice. "Let me guess, Lady Carrol told you that I need someone to be seen with in public, a little doll to carry around with me?"

There was an edge to his voice, one that I immediately recognized as the spite felt by an heir with too much to bear. My heart twisted for him, but I kept my answer proper. "Lady Carrol said that I would be an excellent Bloodletter for you, sir."

The Prince let out a humorless laugh. "I bet," He said. He stopped circling me and looked me in the eye. His eyes were such a dark shade of brown that they appeared black in the low light. "And what do you think?"

I was taken aback by his question. I took a breath before replying. "Your Majesty, I come from a wealthy family in Wythtir and I know firsthand the pressures that are faced by young nobility. If there is anyone who would be the best Bloodletter for you, it is me."

The Prince smirked and turned for the door. "We'll see about that."

∞

Three days later, the Prince had not returned.

The maid who tended to my room was named Judy. I had wrestled her name out of her the next day, and she hadn't spoken to me since. I slept the days away, with nothing and no one to keep me entertained. I found myself wishing for any sort of company. Training from Lady Carrol or even a childish argument with Greta would have been a pleasure.

When Judy came in with my lunch, I cornered her. "Judy!"

The maid peeped and hid her face with her hands.

"Judy, I know you're instructed not to get to know me, and that's fine," I said, exasperated. "But please, answer my questions."

Judy peeked over her fingers. "Yes, miss?"

"Where is the Prince?"

"Prince Edmund?" Judy asked for confirmation. When I nodded, she continued with a sigh. "His Majesty is very busy, he is the Heir Apparent, after all. The Crown Prince has daily lessons, meetings, social events." She rattled them off on her fingers.

"I am well aware of that. But does he not need blood?"

Judy went white. "Yes, of course, Miss."

"Then why has he not come for mine?"

Judy blushed. "Why do you want him to so badly?" She looked at me suspiciously.

I rolled my eyes. "Because I'm bored, Judy!" I screamed, my frustration bubbling over. "I've done nothing but sit in this room for days. I've been here in the palace for nearly a month and I've done nothing but get dressed up, eat and sleep. Surely the Prince has another Bloodletter that I could at least talk to?"

Judy shook her head, going another shade of red. "No, that would not be proper, Miss. Prince Edmund's other Bloodletter is a man."

I clenched my teeth. I had no idea that a co-ed Blood House was so scandalous.

"And, if you promise to keep this between us, Miss." Judy waited for me to nod before continuing to whisper. "The Prince, he won't be seeing you often. Only for social events. He, um, well, he prefers the male blood."

TWENTY-ONE

JUDY WAS RIGHT. Two more lonely days passed before I couldn't bear it a second longer.

Late that night, I crept out of my room and made my way through the dark twisting hallways until I found the library. I was unsurprised to find the room dark and empty. I grabbed a book at random and snuck up to the second level. I settled into a corner, reading in the warm glow of a single lamp.

I had become immersed in a lighthearted narrative about a band of travelers when the sound of the door opening alerted me.

I crept over to the railing and saw Prince Isaac lighting a lamp and sitting in an armchair. A heavy book rested on his lap and a handful of loose papers were stacked on the table beside him. He was muttering to himself softly, looking from the notes and back to the book, his fingers tracing the lines of text.

I retreated from the edge, carefully weighing my options. One, I could sit up here and read, waiting for him to leave. Or two, I could go down and speak to him, then leave. He hadn't minded last time he found me in the library, though Bloodletters were forbidden to leave their rooms.

I drummed my fingers against the leather cover of the book in my hands. For the first time as long as I could remember, my hands weren't unbearably cold.

After only a moment of deliberation, I decided on option two. My unbearable loneliness won out against common sense. I had only stepped on the first step when the Prince looked up. Even in the dim light, he looked as handsome as ever.

"Ah, can't sleep either, huh?" The Prince asked with a smile.

I was taken aback by his casual tone. "Yes, I have been confined to my room and couldn't stand it any longer."

Prince Isaac nodded, rising to meet me at the bottom of the spiral staircase. He held his hand out to me.

It took me a moment to realize his gesture and placed my hand in his. He kissed it softly before letting it go. His grip was strong and warm. I held my book to my chest to disguise my trembling.

"I heard that they promoted you," Prince Isaac said, returning to his chair and gesturing for me to join him.

I sat nervously. "Promoted?"

"To be my brother's Bloodletter," the Prince clarified and laughed at my expression. "Ah, so it's true then. How's that going for you?"

I resisted the urge to be brutally honest. "It has been uneventful, thus far."

The Prince laughed again. "How polite of you," he said and sat back in the armchair, studying me for a moment before continuing. "I know my brother can be quite the bore, but be happy about that, at least he won't be draining you."

I forced a smile, and he laughed again. "Actually, the Prince and I have not gotten to know each other yet. Though, I'm sure he's charming," I said.

Isaac snorted. "You'll learn soon enough."

"So, what about you, can you not sleep either?" I asked, changing the subject to avoid any hot water. Bloodletter training had been helpful in these circumstances, always twisting the conversation away from yourself.

The Prince shrugged. "You could say that. I often study late into the night."

I nodded, another familiar feeling, though I could not say so out loud. I nodded towards to book. "What are you reading?"

Prince Isaac glanced down at the thick book sitting on the table. "History, mostly. Sometimes I change it up and read some military strategy or economics. Right now, I'm focusing on the reign of my great grandfather. I was young when he passed, but there's no shortage of literature about him."

I nodded. "King Ronald Saxon. The king who introduced the Bloodletting Regulation Act."

The Prince cocked an eyebrow. "Beautiful and well read, who would have known?" He smiled.

I shrugged off the compliment. "I had plenty of history lessons in my previous life," I said and bowed my head modestly.

"Hm," Prince Isaac paused. "I heard rumors that you came from a wealthy family. Do you care to share who?"

I went rigid, my heart pounding in my chest. Violet Ackerman was dead. "No, it's too painful," I whispered.

The Prince nodded. "Alright," he conceded.

"Forgive me, sir," I said after a beat of silence. "But why are you up studying all night? Are you not tutored all day; you must be exhausted?"

Prince Isaac's expression darkened, and I immediately regretted my question. "No," he said finally. "I am not tutored all day. I did the usual schooling, but now that I am an adult, my father insists that I focus more on military matters," He paused. "After all, I am not the heir."

I blinked, unsure of how to respond. I felt a chill run through me and had to look away from the Prince. "I see. I'm sorry."

The Prince shook his head. "Don't worry about it, there's nothing you can do about it."

My eyes met his, and I felt myself being drawn closer to him. I blinked and inched away. "Well, I best be getting back to my room," I said as I got to my feet.

Prince Isaac bolted up, reached out, and grabbed my hand lightly. "Wait."

I looked at him, eyes wide. No one in this palace had even dared make physical contact with me. Servants sidestepped me and looked down, not wanting to get attached. His skin was warm against mine.

The Prince immediately released me. "I apologize." He clasped his hands behind his back. "I just wanted to ask you – will you be here tomorrow?"

I tried to suppress my smile. The Prince wanted to spend time with me? After weeks of nothing but loneliness, I would have been a fool not to take him up on his offer. As a reading partner, perhaps. Nothing that would get us in trouble. I nodded. "I will."

Prince Isaac smiled. "Great, I'll look forward to it."

I bowed my head and hurried out of the library, hiding a grin behind the book in my hand.

∞

Judy worked wordlessly as she helped me dress for another meaningless day. She cinched me up in an emerald green dress and pinned my hair. She was getting better at managing the unruly amber curls.

The maid left, and I was alone again. I sat by the window, reading the book I had taken from the library last night. I wanted to finish it today to ensure that I had a reason to return to the library besides visiting the Prince. I stared at the page but couldn't absorb the words, my mind was elsewhere. Lost in the memory of his emerald green eyes, the same shade as the dress I wore.

Will you be here tomorrow?

I sighed and pressed the book to my chest. I gazed out the window, watching the groundskeepers clearing snow from the paths again. It was nearing mid-February and the snow was still falling in full force. I wondered if I would be allowed to explore the grounds once the weather improved. Maybe on the arm of Prince Isaac, walking and flirting in the gardens.

No. I forced myself to abandon those fantasies. That was just silly. He was the Prince and I was only a Bloodletter, and his brother's Bloodletter at that. I doubted that it was proper for us even to see each other as much as he already had.

I read until lunchtime. There was a knock at the door, and I called them in, thinking it would be Judy with my lunch.

Lady Carrol appeared instead. Her cheeks were rosy, and her dark hair had been piled on top of her head, giving her the appearance that she was taller than she was. She fanned her face and composed herself before speaking. She must have run up from a lower floor. "Good afternoon, Violet."

I snapped the book shut and hid it behind me. "Good afternoon, ma'am." I bowed my head to her.

"I'm happy to see you are doing well," Lady Carrol said. "I came to inform you that there will be a ball held this weekend. His Majesty will need a Bloodletter to accompany him, so please prepare yourself accordingly."

"A ball?" I stammered. "What is the occasion?"

"The Annual Valentine's Ball, my dear," she replied. She flung open my wardrobe and combed through the dressed. "I don't see anything in here that will be suitable," she muttered. "I'll send the dressmaker over this afternoon."

I stood, slipping the book under a pillow. I didn't want her to know I had been sneaking off to the library. "I'm positive there's something, please don't go through the trouble," I protested. I hated being fitted for dresses. It was a long, boring ordeal and my feet ached by the end. To make matters worse, the dressmaker didn't talk much, so it was hours of unbearable silence and pin pricks.

"Oh, I must!" Lady Carrol insisted. "His Majesty is about the age to be married and he has yet to find a suitable bride. Your appearance and performance are just as important as his."

I clenched my teeth. "No pressure." I mumbled under my breath as she slammed the wardrobe shut.

Lady Carrol looked me up and down. "I will call for the dressmaker immediately. Try not to eat too much at lunch, we want to make sure the measurements are accurate."

I bit back a sarcastic comment, and I bowed my head as she left. "Of course, my Lady."

∞

As expected, the fitting took forever, and it was well into the evening before she finally released me. I finished the book and ate ravenously at dinner after skipping lunch for the sake of fashion.

At midnight, I quietly slipped out of my room and made my way to the library. The hallways were empty as usual. When I entered the library, I found the Prince already there. He was sitting in a chair with a stack of books beside him.

Prince Isaac looked up. "Ah, there you are, I was worried that you might not be coming."

I felt my cheeks tingle with heat. "I wouldn't break a promise to you, Your Majesty." I bowed my head.

The Prince stood and took the book from my hand. He tossed it onto a nearby chair and kissed my knuckles. "Please, you can drop the formalities."

I blushed deeper, pulling my hands away and holding them behind my back. "I couldn't. It wouldn't be proper."

Prince Isaac rolled his eyes and put his hands into his pockets. The top button of his shirt was undone, and I could see the notch of his throat. "My entire life has been nothing but formalities," He said. "And if you are comfortable about breaking Bloodletter curfew and taking books from my family's private library, I highly doubt that this should make a difference."

I looked away from his piercing gaze. He stepped closer to me and I could feel the heat radiating from him.

"Just try it," he said. "Say my name."

My lips trembled. "Isaac." His name tasted sinful on my tongue. My body felt as if it were on fire.

"See, that wasn't so bad," Isaac said. He touched my cheek and our eyes met. "And now, I believe you haven't even told me your name yet."

I flinched. If I told him my name, he would know I was the Bloodletter from the Autumn Festival. What would he think? Would he ever remember?

Isaac watched me, patiently waiting.

The Prince was so close to me now. My entire body was trembling. I hadn't been this close to a man since my drunken escapades in the Manor in Wythtir. My old life, where I had teased suitors and broken hearts.

"Violet." I let it out in a rush, speaking in a whisper as if it were a terrible secret.

"Violet?" Isaac repeated. He took a step back and examined me carefully. He reached out and wrapped a tendril of my hair around his long fingers. "I knew it

was you. I knew I recognized you from somewhere."
He said. Even though he was whispering, the silence
of the library amplified his voice.

I nodded. "Yes, we met at the Autumn Festival."

Isaac's eyes blazed. "Yes, I remember now. The
woman that I saved from the Baron. The woman with
the delicious blood."

I let myself be pulled into his arms. I longed for his
touch, but I would not dare make a move. Instead, I
relaxed and let his strength consume me. This wasn't
right, I couldn't silence my mind. If someone were to
walk in, I would be done for.

"I never forgot that taste," Isaac said, his mouth
next to my ear.

I shivered. My heart was pounding with the thrill.
This was wrong. I was a Bloodletter, and I wasn't even
his Bloodletter. I summoned my resolve and gently
pushed out of his grip. "I'm sorry, Your Majesty, but
we shouldn't."

"Isaac," He interrupted me.

"Isaac," I conceded. "We shouldn't be acting like
this."

"I know," the Prince said. "You're my brother's
Bloodletter, we shouldn't be seen together at all." He
paused, chuckling to himself. "Not that my brother
would know what to do with a beautiful woman
anyway."

It took all of myself control not to fling myself at
him at that moment. I had no doubt that he could teach

me a thing or two about how he could handle a woman. I shook my head. "Well, I should be going." I reached for the door handle. "And I think it would be better if we didn't see each other again," I added.

Isaac put his hand on the door. The strength of a Royal was not one I could overcome, even if I pulled at the handle with all my might. "Please don't go," he said earnestly.

"I can't stay, Isaac." I said. I pulled at the door handle. My eyes flicked up to his face, and I leaned forward, kissing him with more passion than I had ever felt in my life. He kissed me back, releasing the door and holding onto my shoulders. I tightened my grip on the door handle and broke away from this kiss.

I held our gaze for a moment longer. "Goodbye," I breathed and dashed out of the library before he could stop me.

TWENTY-TWO

I DID NOT RETURN TO THE LIBRARY FOR THE REST OF THE WEEK.

I spent my time in my room, trying to pen a letter to Amelia and tearing up the paper halfway through every time. I wanted to tell her everything, but I knew if the letter was intercepted, I would have to answer to the Royals. Her romantic heart would have burst, as she said, it was like a fairy tale. But fairy tales weren't real. Even if Isaac and I were to fall madly in love, there would be no happy ending for us. It was better this way, I thought, even if I could never return to the library after dark.

I spent the day of the ball preparing. I woke at dawn to be bathed, groomed, dressed and painted for the event. Lady Carrol briefed me as the maids worked silently.

"Tonight is the biggest night of the Winter season. Many eligible ladies will make their debut and the Prince is expected to dance with as many of them as possible," Lady Carrol explained as she paced back and forth.

I sucked in a breath as Judy tied my corset.

"The King and Queen have felt pressure to get him married off before the next Autumn festival. Noble families are starting to talk, and that can put the ruling family in a perilous position," Lady Carrol continued.

Of course, it would. The Royals were ruthless. If any ruling family showed weakness, the people would begin to doubt their power. It was not unlike the pressures that the Ministers' families felt. Another reason that my father would have never kept a female heir, not when he had two perfectly good sons going to waste. I wiggled into my dress with the help of Judy and a nameless maid who I hadn't seen before.

The dress was bright red, the color of fresh blood. It was made of silk taffeta with a full bustle and train. It pooled at my feet and came up to my chest in an arched sweetheart neckline. My neck and shoulders were on full display, as was the style for Bloodletters. The maids started to work on my hair next.

"Now for you, young lady, you must be a vision of elegance and poise. I'm sure this will be no trouble for you, considering your upbringing. Have you attended a Royal Ball before?"

I nodded, ignoring the tuts of the maids. "Yes, ma'am. I attended the Autumn Festival Ball as a Bloodletter for Madam Desjardins."

"Good," Lady Carrol marked something down on the papers she was holding. "Most of the same rules apply. Don't speak unless you are spoken to, stand straight and smile, but don't flirt. Your job is to make the Crown Prince look his best. If anyone else asks you for blood, you must politely decline. You are only for His Majesty."

I nodded.

"There will be other Bloodletters there for the esteemed guests," Lady Carrol added. "You are to stay by Prince Edmund's side unless he is dancing with a Lady. In which case you are to stand by the side and make yourself available once he is done. There are two hundred confirmed guests, so try to keep your eye on him."

"Yes, ma'am."

Lady Carrol sighed happily and looked me up and down. "You will be fantastic. I only hope that your beauty does not distract from the eligible ladies."

I blushed. "I don't think that will be a problem, my Lady."

"Hm," Lady Carrol walked around me once again, tapping her chin as she thought. "Judy, make sure her makeup is modest."

"Yes, ma'am," Judy said, tying my hair with more force than usual.

I winced, watching them work in the mirror. I set my shoulders and let Lady Carrol drone on and on about every detail. I was already looking forward to the night being over.

∞

There was a deep pocket in the side of my dress for me to keep my Bloodletting tools. As I was intended to only be used by Prince Edmund, the usual contraption of needle and tubing was not required. This also meant that I was permitted to wear shorter gloves. I looked at my inner arms. There was no sign of scars or bruising. It had been so long since I last gave blood. I was beginning to forget what it felt like.

I could hear music echoing from the ballroom. Most of the guests had already arrived. I was waiting in the antechamber for Prince Edmund. I paced around, the rustling of my skirts and clicking of my heels on the marble floor became a rhythm.

The King and Queen had already been announced. Prince Edmund should have been here by now. I wondered if Isaac would be announced. The memories of his touch and his kiss set my skin on fire.

Someone opened the door and cleared their throat.

I opened my eyes, more than slightly disappointed to see Prince Edmund and not Isaac. I bowed my head low. "Good evening, Your Majesty."

Prince Edmund looked less than thrilled to be here. He was dressed in a black three-piece suit. His white pocket square was embroidered with the crest of the House of Strix. His dark hair was freshly trimmed. His round face and soft dark eyes made it hard to believe that he was the eldest of the two brothers. Isaac was commanding and confident while Edmund was quiet and unremarkable.

I smiled my best smile, eager to get the night over with and return to my room.

Edmund held out his arm for me. "Let's get this over with." He muttered.

I nodded and slipped my arm around his. We stepped into the ballroom and my breath caught in my throat. As Lady Carrol promised, the room was filled with guests, the most influential Royals dressed in their finest winter jewel tones mixed with black and shades of gray. The ballroom was decorated with golden trim and large mirrors, the vaulted ceiling painted and illuminated by glittering chandeliers. The chamber orchestra quieted as the Prince was announced.

"Ladies and Gentlemen, may I present his Royal Highness, Prince Edmund, Crown Prince of Inwaed."

The attendees turned in our direction. I remembered to stay half a step behind him as we descended the stairs. There was applause. I could feel the energy in the room shift. Mothers were whispering in their daughter's ears.

The musicians took up their instruments and began playing a waltz.

I breathed a sigh of relief as the guests returned to their conversation. I followed Edmund to the dais where the King and Queen waited. King Luther stood stoic, watching the guests.

Queen Leona pulled her son into a warm hug. "I'm glad you finally showed up. Lady Mauldin has been eyeing the door all night. Her daughter is first on your card, right?" Prince Edmund looked like his mother, the same dark hair and soft features.

I tried not to listen as she gave advice to the Prince. They sounded so desperate to get him married off. I stared at the floor, waiting for Prince Edmund. It sounded like he would have a busy night of dances ahead of him. In a way, I felt sorry for him. I was no stranger to the pressures of being an heir. Before my mother died, every gala was a performance. There was no room for mistakes.

Queen Leona finally released her son. She glanced at me and I lowered my eyes again. I hated their appraising looks; I could feel the Royals' eyes on me as Edmund took me by the arm again and went out to mingle with the guests.

After some small talk, the Prince was approached by a pretty girl that I safely assumed to be Lady Mauldin's daughter. Her face was glowing with excitement as she curtsied. "Your Majesty."

I hid a grimace. Her desperation was obvious. I stood by a wall as Edmund danced with her. I clasped my hands behind my back and watched him twirl around the ballroom. He was a good dancer, but unenthusiastic. His boredom was obvious.

The night dragged on and Edmund was kept busy with dance after dance. I shifted and leaned against the wall to ease the pain in my feet. I noticed that the crowd was beginning to thin. Some of the younger Royals had wandered off in pairs or groups. I sighed, remembering those days myself. Stuffy occasions were no place for teenagers, I guess it was true for the Royals as well.

The orchestra stopped for a break and Edmund returned to my side. He looked exhausted.

"Your Majesty, are you feeling ok?" I asked.

Edmund waved away my concern. "Fine." He picked a glass of champagne from a passing server.

I glanced around the ballroom. There were about a dozen Bloodletters stationed around the room and they were all busy with customers. "Would you like some blood, sir?"

Edmund's eyes perked up for a moment before his indifferent mask fell into place. He looked at me, his eyes trailing down my arm. "No, thank you." I didn't miss the hint of disgust in his voice. "Why don't you go back to your room? I don't need you here."

I bristled, feeling heat rush to my face. I bit the inside of my cheek to keep my emotions under control. What was the point of being his Bloodletter if he refused to drink from me? I was insulted. I had given up my freedom for the Saxons, groomed to be a perfect Bloodletter, and he wouldn't even give me a chance. I opened my mouth to argue, but the orchestra began to play again.

"Excuse me," Edmund said, glancing at his dance card. He left to entertain another young lady in a giant sparkling gown.

I glared at the back of his head and crossed my arms. This was such a waste of my time; I could have been reading.

"Now that's no way for a beautiful woman to look. You'll get wrinkles."

I bolted upward, letting my hands fall to my sides. Prince Isaac had snuck against the wall, his hand nearly touching mine. "Your Majesty," I hissed. "What are you doing here?"

Prince Isaac raised his eyebrows. "I thought we talked about this."

I set my jaw and faced forward. "Isaac," I corrected myself. "And I thought I said that we couldn't see each other anymore."

"Well, this is the Valentine's Ball. Even the lowly spare has to make an appearance."

"I didn't hear you being announced."

Isaac chuckled bitterly. "They wouldn't, tonight is all about finding a girl for my beloved big brother."

I watched Prince Edmund dancing around the ballroom. "Yeah, I noticed. Poor guy hasn't had a break all night."

Isaac didn't sound sympathetic. "Well, he should just hurry up and pick one." He leaned against the wall, edging closer to me. "As for you, why don't we get out of here?"

I blushed and turned my face away from him, focusing on the orchestra. "No, I don't think so. I need to be here in case Edmund…"

"Needs your blood?" Isaac whispered. "Believe me, he won't." He brushed his hand against mine. "I believe I could put it to much better use."

I nearly fainted. I turned to face him; he was so close. "What is it about you that is so intoxicating?"

Isaac smirked. "You tell me."

I looked around the ballroom, but no one was paying attention to us. "We could get into a lot of trouble."

"I know." Isaac said, taking my hand and lacing my fingers through his. "Come on, let's go and have some real fun."

Before I could change my mind, I nodded, and the Prince led me to the doors, staying on the edge of the crowd. No one even bothered to glance at us. If Edmund went looking for me, he would assume I took his offer and went back to my room for the night.

Holding tightly to Isaac's hand, I followed him through the dark halls, down the stairs and to a wing of the palace I had never been to before. "Where are we going?" I whispered, clutching the hem of my skirt to stop myself from tripping.

"You'll see." Isaac looked over his shoulder and smiled.

A warmth spread through me. He was so handsome. He was supposed to be untouchable, and yet here we were together, running through the halls like lovesick characters from a romance novel. I really should write to Amelia.

We stopped at a set of double doors. Isaac turned to me, his hands resting gently on my bare shoulders. "Ok, what you're about to see, you can't speak of to anyone. Even Edmund."

I nodded, glancing around nervously.

Isaac opened the doors, and we slipped into a dimly lit room. It was a sitting room filled with the dozen or more younger Royals who had disappeared during the ball. They were lounging on chairs, sipping glasses of wine. Someone was playing the piano, a soft melodic tune. They were chattering and giggling amongst themselves. The women had loosened their corsets and kicked their shoes off in the corner. The men's ties hung lose around their necks. They looked so normal. Like average teenagers, finally free from the critical eyes of their parents.

Everyone looked up when we walked in. I tensed nervously. Isaac kept a hand on my shoulder.

"Ladies and Gentlemen, may I present his Royal Lowness, Prince Isaac the Spare Prince of Inwaed." A young man shouted across the room and the rest of the attendees broke into laughter. "Oh, and let's not forget our lovely Bloodletter." The man jumped up from his chair and posed in an exaggerated bow.

Isaac waved them off. "Yeah, yeah, thank you Horace."

Horace grinned and passed Isaac a glass of wine. The chatter started again, and the pianist picked up the tempo.

Isaac took a sip of wine before introducing me to his friend. "Horace, I'd like you to meet Violet."

Horace kissed my knuckles. "Charmed. It's a pleasure to meet the lady that Isaac hasn't been able to stop talking about."

I glanced at Isaac and noticed a pink tinge in his cheeks. "Thank you," I said, taking a glass of wine from him as well. I drank deeply, I had not been able to touch a drop of wine since coming to the House of Strix. Alcohol thinned the blood and lowered inhibitions – a combination that was not healthy for a Bloodletter. It tasted glorious, a full-bodied red. I was not surprised that Royals favored red over white.

"I've missed you," Isaac said to me once Horace turned his attention elsewhere.

"It's only been a week." I replied.

"Yes, but after that kiss, you're all I could think about." Isaac said. "I waited in the library every night for you."

"I'm a woman of my word; I told you that we shouldn't be together."

"And yet here you are." Isaac sipped his wine. His hand wandered up my arm and on my shoulder. "You're so beautiful, Violet."

"Is that the wine talking?"

"Never. I only speak the truth to you." Isaac whispered.

I shivered. I craved more of his touch, even sitting beside me he was too far away.

Before I could speak, the door opened again, and a girl ran in with a violin. "Got one!" She raised it over her head victoriously.

The guests cheered and whooped.

Isaac grinned. "Good, I was wondering when this party was going to get started."

The girl went to the pianist's side and whispered in his ear. He nodded eagerly and broke out into an upbeat song. She played along with him, not missing a beat and dancing in her stiff silk gown. One by one, the others got to their feet and began to dance. This was no typical ballroom dance, but one that required much more physical contact. They laughed, sang and held each other, twisting and jumping in ways that would make their parents blush.

I stood watching the young Royals, holding onto my empty wineglass tightly. I had never seen anything like this before.

Isaac nudged his elbow into my side. "Want to dance?"

"I, I," I stammered. "I don't believe I've had enough wine for that."

"Don't be shy," the Prince said. He leaned close to me in order to be heard over the music. "Let's have a little fun. Tomorrow you're going to be shut into your room again, waiting for a Royal who will never want your blood."

I bit down on my lip. He was right. I needed to take this chance. "Alright." I said, slamming the glass down and jumping up from my chair. "Let's do it."

Prince Isaac didn't look the least bit surprised. He took my hand and led me into the middle of the room. The chairs and sofas had been cleared away to make room for the dancing bodies. It was hot in here; make up smeared, hair fell flat and clothing wrinkled. A party unlike any I had ever seen.

Isaac pulled me against him. His body was hard against mine as we danced.

It took me a few moments to get into the beat, feeling the music moving through my blood. We danced until my feet burned. I kicked off my shoes, hiked up my skirt and danced. I never wanted to let him go. I had never felt as free in my entire life as I did then.

I wrapped my arms around his shoulders, pulling myself up to his face. I didn't have to wait long; the Prince kissed me in the middle of the crowd and my heart burst. I didn't care what any of them might be thinking. I was a Bloodletter, being kissed by a Royal in the middle of his peers. They were all caught up in the moment to give it a second glance.

Isaac growled against my cheek; his eyes were burning. "You're amazing, Violet," he whispered. His grip tightened on my waist and I felt his true strength.

I brushed the pale blond hair from his face and kissed him again. No words I could say would be enough. Even with all the reading I had done, all the lessons I had completed, there were no words for how I felt that night. It was all so new, so exhilarating, I never wanted it to end.

When we broke away from yet another kiss, I noticed the fire in his eyes. It was the same as any other Royal had when they needed blood. I had been trained to recognize it and I found myself wanting to give it to him. "You need blood." I whispered into his ear.

Isaac's hands froze on my waist. He cleared his throat and blinked. "No, I'm ok." He said.

"You're lying." I pressed myself against him. "I can take care of it for you. You said yourself that my blood was the best you'd ever tasted."

Isaac swallowed hard.

I wasn't sure if it was the wine weakening my resolve, but I wanted to give him my blood. I needed to. I needed to feel the release, the rush of pain. I reached into my pocket and withdrew the needle.

"No," Isaac said. His mouth and his eyes told different stories. "If I do, I'll never be able to have another's again. You can't do this."

"Do you want my blood, Isaac?"

Isaac's lips trembled. "Yes, more than anything."

"Then don't deny yourself, it's just one night. No one will know." I wanted more this time. I wanted to feel his lips against my skin. I wanted him to take me how they used to, before all the regulations and health codes. I wanted to feel the beast in him. I grazed the sharp end of the needle along my shoulder. Red bubbles of blood spouted up along the line.

Isaac hissed and plunged forward, pressing his mouth against my skin and licking the blood from the wound.

My vision blurred. I hung onto him as hard as he clutched me, letting him drink the life from my veins. It wasn't a deep cut; the flow wouldn't last for long. It was just enough to replenish his energy and to let me feel his body against mine.

I felt the shift inside of him. A raw animal-like desire. The fire that burned inside of him, growing hotter than the sun itself. This is what true power was. This is what it meant to be a Royal. To have every mortal at your mercy. To be a God on earth.

I grinned against his cheek as he pulled away, breathing heavily.

I had given him my blood; it was only a matter of time before he gave me his.

TWENTY-THREE

MY BORING WORLD SHIFTED THAT NIGHT.

I slept in the day and waited anxiously for midnight. After the servants and staff had retired to their beds, I slipped out of my room and met Isaac in the library. I was no longer bored, wasting away while I wanted Edmund to show interest in me. For the first time in a long time, I began to look forward to tomorrow.

Dressed in a gauzy blue gown, I entered the library and shut the door behind me, twisting the lock closed with a click.

"I was wondering when you were going to show up."

I found Isaac sprawled on a sofa, surrounded by a pile of books.

"I'm sorry," I said, taking a seat beside him. "The staff wasn't quick to leave tonight."

"All that matters is that you're here now." Isaac pulled me to him and kissed me. He brushed a stray curl from my eyes and ran his fingers along my cheek gently.

Though the time we spent together had only been brief, I knew without a doubt that there was something special between us. It was something that I had never felt before. I penned a letter to Amelia, trying to keep my words discrete in case the letter was opened before leaving the palace. I was counting on her advice to help me. She was the hopeless romantic. I had laughed at her for it before, but now I was seeing the appeal.

I noticed a bruise on the Prince's arm, half visible under his rolled-up shirt sleeve. "What happened?"

Isaac glanced at the purple bruise. "Oh. That. I fell off my horse this afternoon during training," He laughed. "Don't worry about me. Royals heal quickly. It'll be gone before breakfast tomorrow."

Strength, longevity, beauty and power. That was what it meant to be a Royal. The more time I spent with Isaac, the more I cursed myself for being born a commoner. I kissed him and he returned it to me passionately.

Our kisses grew hot and demanding. I straddled him, deliberately choosing a light dress with no petticoats or corset for this reason. It took too long to get out of. His kisses ran down my neck and shoulders, his hands exploring and clutching my body.

"Did you lock the door?" He asked.

"Of course." I breathed in a break between kisses. My hands were trembling. I couldn't get enough of him. His body. His lust. His power.

"Excellent," The Prince growled in the back of his throat and pinned me down to the plush sofa.

When our lovemaking came to an end, Isaac cradled me in his arms.

I tried in vain to tame my shaking hands and button up my bodice. "Do you need blood, Isaac?" I whispered.

Isaac's grip tightened on me a fraction. "No," He said finally and eased back. "I had some earlier," He avoided my gaze before continuing. "If I don't use my Bloodletters, someone will get suspicious."

I clenched my teeth and nodded. I hated knowing that he was drinking from someone else, but it was part of the deal. No one could know about us. It was not unheard of for Royals to pursue physical relationships with their Bloodletters – but Isaac was a Prince and I was his brother's Bloodletter. It would cause a scandal and the ruling family didn't need any more doubts or rumors about Edmund.

I traced a finger on his chest. His skin was flushed. "I understand."

"You know that I care for you, right?"

I met his eyes. "Yes."

"Good," Isaac said. He kissed my temple and rose from the sofa. Once he was dressed, he went back to his pile of books.

I tilted to my head to read the titles written in gold leaf on the spine of the leather-bound books. They were mostly history books again. "Don't you ever get tired of studying? Don't you read fiction?"

"I used to when I was younger," Isaac replied. He found the thick volume he was looked for and leafed through the pages. "But now I do it to teach myself."

"You said that your parents want you to focus on military training, why is that?" I tucked my legs up to my chest.

"Well, Edmund is the heir. It's up to him to rule one day; make babies, wave at the masses, and dance in balls." Isaac shrugged. "I'll be a figurehead for the army."

"But Inwaed hasn't known war for centuries, why bother?"

"To keep me out of trouble, I suspect," Isaac mumbled. His face brightened, and he smiled at me. "Though, to be honest, I've been doing a lot less reading since you came around."

I blushed. "Do you think Edmund wants to be King one day?" I asked after a moment.

Isaac looked surprised. "Well, even if he didn't," he answered carefully. "That is his destiny. So, he'd best get himself a bride and learn to live with his fate." He set the book down. It was titled THE ROYAL BLOODLINES.

About an hour later, I left the library. While I could sleep the morning away, Prince Isaac could not. I admired him for all the effort that he put into being a prince, even if he was only a spare, as he referred to himself. I wondered if Edmund was as serious as Isaac was. In the two times I had met Edmund, he seemed withdrawn and unhappy with his luxurious lifestyle. I suspected it was just the pressure of finding a suitable bride that was bearing down on him.

I wished that Prince Edmund would come by my room at least once in a while to check in on me; it would be the polite thing to do. I wondered if there was any way for me to become Prince Isaac's Bloodletter instead. Or more, perhaps. His bride? I shook my head and turned a corner. That was just stupid. We would never be able to be together.

"Do you really think you have a chance?"

I looked up from the carpet. I had been caught up in my own thoughts, I hadn't noticed someone standing against the wall. Greta.

"Greta?" I hissed. "What are you doing here?"

Greta smirked and tossed her loose hair over her shoulder. She was wrapped up in a long dressing gown. "I should ask you the same thing."

"Why aren't you in the Bloodletter's wing? And in your nightclothes too!" I looked her up and down.

"Says you," Greta motioned at my disheveled gown. "I know what you're doing."

I flushed red. "Doing what?"

Greta took a sauntering step towards me. She had a familiar look in her eyes, the cocky, conniving one that she wore nearly all the time when we lived with Madam Desjardins. "You're seeing Prince Isaac." She grinned.

"What proof do you have?" I spat.

"Well, you're not the only one who gets bored in this palace," Greta said, leaning forward to whisper. "I saw you both leave the ball."

I jerked away from her. "You weren't there!"

"Ha! In case you forgot, I am a staff Bloodletter. You couldn't take your eyes off Isaac, so I'm not surprised you didn't see me."

The ballroom had been full of over two hundred people, of course I hadn't seen her. "I was doing my job for Prince Edmund. I wasn't looking at anyone else."

"Right, sure you were." Greta rolled her eyes. "I wonder what Lady Carrol would say if I told her that you were stealing away with the Prince's brother?" She mused. "And meeting him in the dead of night in the library to do who knows what."

I clenched my fists. "You're not supposed to be out after dark either," I said. "You couldn't tell even if there was something worth telling. I was reading."

"So, you're sneaking into the library to study chastely with the Prince? Forgive me if I don't believe you." Greta ignored my comment.

I rolled my eyes and shouldered past her. "Shut up, Greta. Get back where you belong."

Greta made a disgusted sound in her throat. "Excuse me?" She hissed as loud as she could without alerting the staff. She stomped after me and seized my arm.

I ripped it away from her. "Don't touch me."

"You must think you're something special, don't you?" Greta sneered. "Let me tell you something, Violet. You're nothing to them. You're nothing to him. You're nothing but a source of food for these Royals. That's all you'll ever be." She spoke over my protest. "And let me tell you something else, if anyone finds out that you're sneaking out at night to study anatomy with the Prince – well, I wouldn't be surprised if that was the end of you." She spun on her heel and walked away.

I watched her leave, seething with rage. How dare she assume the Prince's feelings towards me? I wanted to chase her, punish her for her rudeness. But what could I do? I had to think of something before she let out the secret to Lady Carrol. Greta was right about one thing, if I was caught, there would be hell to pay.

∞

The next evening when Judy brought me my dinner, I heard keys jingle in her pocket. Every staff

239

member must have a master key. I drummed my fingers on the table as the maid laid out another plentiful meal. If I could get my hands on the key, then I could confront Greta on my own terms. I bit my lip and stretched, knocking a bowl of soup onto the floor.

Judy shrieked; the soup was steaming hot.

"Oh no!" I exclaimed. "Judy, are you alright?" I bent down to help her clean up the mess, locking my fingers around the keys in the pocket of her apron. I stuffed them down my sleeve.

In the clamor, Judy didn't notice the lightness of her pocket. "No, please, I'll take care of it."

"Let me help you," I insisted.

Once the soup was cleaned up, Judy smoothed her hair and took the dishes away. "My apologies again, Miss. Shall I get you another bowl?"

I shook my head. "No, it's quite alright," I said. "Have a good evening, Judy."

The maid blinked. "Yes, you too." She took the cart away and left.

I pulled the keys from my sleeve after the sounds of her footsteps had faded away. There were three keys on the ring, each gleaming in the light. I set them on the table in front of me and stared at them while I finished my dinner.

I wouldn't be meeting Isaac tonight. He had mentioned last night to me that his family was off to a party and that he was very sorry that he'd have to spend his time at a table full of stuffy Royals than with me.

My heart longed for his touch, but my body needed a break from the exhaustion of sneaking out nightly. I dressed for bed and hid the keys in my bedside table. I lay awake for a while, staring up at the ceiling. The fireplace crackled merrily on the other side of the room and the warmth eventually lulled me to sleep.

My restful sleep turned into a slew of nightmares, pulling and picking at my skin. Holding me down and taking my blood, my life, my soul. When I finally escaped their clutches, I awoke trembling and sweating. I looked around my room wildly, unable to remember exactly what I had been terrorized by in my dream. There were no memories, only fear.

I steadied my breathing, wiping my face with the hem of my nightgown.

Greta. Greta would tell Lady Carrol that I was seeing Prince Isaac after dark. She would tell her that we had stole away from the party and that I had abandoned my one purpose that night.

I gnawed on my bottom lip. I couldn't let her ruin everything that I had worked on. After some time, who knew, I could be more than a Bloodletter to Isaac. After all, his parents weren't exactly paying much attention to him because they were so desperate to keep Edmund's image up.

I couldn't let Greta destroy what little of a life I had left.

I jumped out of bed, wrapped myself in a dressing gown, and pushed my feet into my soft white slippers.

I found the key at the bottom of my bedside table and tucked it inside my sleeve. With the door open a crack, I peeked out to find the hallway was dark and empty as usual. I breathed a sigh of relief and kept to the shadows as I walked from my room to the east wing of the house where the staff Bloodletters were kept.

The journey took longer than I expected. The House of Strix was enormous, and I had barely explored any of it yet. I longed for Spring, when I would hopefully be allowed out on the grounds. Maybe go riding with Isaac. I blushed and shook my head. No. I had to focus on the task at hand.

I would go to Greta and convince her not to open her mouth. She would have to keep my secret. I wished that I had some dirt on her to blackmail her with, but I hadn't associated with her since being promoted to be Edmund's Bloodletter. Our encounter last night reassured me that she probably hadn't changed much. She was the same jealous, manipulative woman that she was when we were with Madam Desjardins.

I got lost a few times on my way to the east wing, but finally found the familiar hallway. I stopped at my old door, wondering if they had filled it already. Then, I looked across the hall to Greta's door. There was no light coming from under the door and it was quiet inside.

I raised my hand to knock, but hesitated. No, she was probably sleeping. I clutched the ring of keys tightly and opened the door myself, luckily getting the right key the first time.

I eased the door open and stuck my head in the room. It was identical to my old room. Greta was asleep in her bed and the fireplace had died down to embers. I slipped inside and shut the door behind me.

Greta sighed in her sleep.

I tiptoed over to the side of her bed. Her bloodletting tools were freshly sanitized and sitting on her bedside table. She must have had a client earlier today. I wondered who the staff Bloodletters worked for, then focused myself back to what needed to be done. I pocketed the keys and watched her for a moment.

Gently, I reached down and grabbed her shoulder.

Greta jumped and squirmed away, gasping and looking around wildly, being torn from a deep sleep. Her eyes fell to me and her fear turned into rage. "What in the Gods' names are you doing in here?" She hissed, scrambling back and covering herself with her quilt.

"I came to make a deal with you." I said, going over the words how I had rehearsed as I walked through the halls.

Greta inched away further, glaring at me. "Get out of my room. Now!"

"Shh," I hissed.

"Do you think I'm going to keep your secret to myself?" Greta spat. "Is that what you came here to do, to keep me quiet?" She laughed. "Nice try. As soon as you're out of the picture, maybe then I'll have a chance to move up here."

"What do you mean out of the picture?"

"Once I tell Lady Carrol, you'll be finished. There's no way they could continue to employ a Bloodletter who is having an affair with a prince. Don't you know better? You're not even on the same level as him. I figured you of all people would understand that. Royals don't see us as anything but a source of food and labor." She cocked an eyebrow. "And maybe something else, in your case."

"Don't act all high and mighty. I know about your own physical relationships with clients back in the Blood House." I said. Anger was bubbling inside me.

Greta sniffed. "That was different. I knew my place." Realization glinted in her eyes. "You think you actually have a chance with him, don't you?"

I clenched my teeth.

"Do you think they'll just forgive that? You'll be dead in a day." Greta added.

I was furious. She was willing to have me killed over jealousy. Somehow, I wasn't surprised. "Not if you're dead first." I mumbled under my breath.

"Sorry, what was that?" Greta sneered.

I looked up and seized her in a flash, grabbing her arms and forcing her down. She shrieked and clawed at me. She was surprisingly strong. I wrestled her down onto the bed and wrapped a hand around her throat.

"What are you doing?" Greta choked.

"Getting rid of the competition." I said through gritted teeth. I tightened my hold on her neck, trying to keep her other hands away from my face. She slapped and scratched at me her words lost in wheezes.

Under my hand her skin was turning red, but she continued to fight back. I grunted, exerting all the pressure I could muster. Strangling someone was harder than I thought it would be. My arms were getting weaker, and she fought with the rabid determination of a trapped animal.

At this rate, she'd survive to tell about my attempt and then I'd surely be done for. What was I thinking? I gritted my teeth. I had started this and now I would have to finish it. I used my knee to hold her body down and swiped the hollow needle from her bedside table.

Protests rattled out of her body. "Wh-what are you doing? Violet! Violet!" She croaked.

"I'm sorry." I whispered and forced the needle deep into her swollen jugular.

Her hand flew to the wound, trying in vain to slow the flow of blood.

I held her body until she finally stilled. The red liquid pulsed out of the hole in her throat. Her blood was all over my white nightclothes, the bed was slick with it. I looked at her glazed eyes and stumbled back away from the bed, looking down at myself.

"What have I done?" I whispered, looking at my bloodstained hands. My entire body was trembling as the adrenaline coursed through me. I took another step back and raised my hand to my face.

I pushed down the guilt.

What was this feeling? Domination. Power. Control. Having the ability to end lives as you felt fit. This was what being a Royal was about, wasn't it?

TWENTY-FOUR

I BURNED MY NIGHTCLOTHES IN THE FIREPLACE AND WENT TO BED.

When Judy came to bring me breakfast, I slipped her keys back into her pocket without her noticing. I sat in my room for the rest of the morning, watching the snow melting and wondering if they knew that I had murdered her.

Shortly after lunch, there was a knock at my door. I had done everything the way I usually did it, taking no more or less care in my appearance, how I acted or what I did to spend my time. I wore long-sleeved dresses to hide the scratches that ran up and down my arms. My heart leaped up into my throat. "Come in," I said and was amazed that I kept my voice steady.

Lady Carrol came in, dressed in green and looking a bit perturbed. "Good afternoon, Violet," she said.

I jumped from my seat and bowed to her. "Good afternoon, ma'am."

"I came to share some unfortunate news," Lady Carrol said. She fidgeted with her hands and clasped them behind her back. "It seems that Greta, the girl from your Blood House, has committed suicide."

I gasped, and thankfully the reaction was correct. I was shocked that they might have come to that conclusion on their own, but the Lady read it as grief. "No!"

Lady Carrol nodded. "I figured you should know, as you were friends."

Friends wasn't really the correct word for it. I nodded solemnly. "What are you going to do about it?" I asked.

Lady Carrol shrugged. "This is quite common unfortunately," She explained. "But we will replace her when there is another Collection." She paused and looked at me. "I'm sorry for your loss." She left without another word.

I collapsed into the chair, holding my hand to my chest. My heart was beating like a drum. That was it then? No investigation? Just written off as a suicide? Did they honestly not care about the lives of the Bloodletters that much? I closed my eyes and hugged myself tightly.

I did the right thing. If I hadn't, it would have been me that would get replaced.

∞

That night, I went to the library to meet Isaac. The Prince had not arrived by the time I got there, so I sat and waited for him. The pile of books by the plush sofa had been left untouched. I curled up and opened one at random.

In the years leading up to the reforms and the Bloodletting Regulation Act, Inwaed had been plunged into chaos and the centuries of peace were at risk. King Ronald Saxon introduced the movement with the help of his Royal advisors, the central government and the Ministers from each of the provinces. Policies were put in place to monitor and regulate Bloodletting, to ensure that diseases would not spread amongst the Royals.

I knew all this by now since my lessons with Heather. I flipped to another random page that had been folded over. A passage had been circled.

Before the Bloodletting Regulation Act, scientists had been working to develop a way to transmit blood from Royals to commoners. In times of disease and unrest, Royals were concerned that their gene pool would grow too small. The Royal bloodlines face many challenges, including infertility. With the added pressure of an ailing population, it was thought that to ensure future generations new Royals would have to be made rather than born.

My mouth went dry. With trembling hands, I turned to the next page.

In order to make a commoner Royal, it is theorized that they must transfuse their blood with that of a Royal. At the time of the experiments, the process was dangerous, and the results were inconclusive.

The door creaked open. I slammed the book shut, tossing it back into the pile.

Isaac looked around the library and smiled at me. "Eager tonight?"

I inched over so he could sit beside me. I wrapped my arms around his shoulders. "I missed you last night."

"Oh, I'm sure you kept busy."

I swallowed hard. "Yes, I did," I said. "But I still had plenty of time to think about you." I discreetly glanced at my nails for the thousandth time that day, just to be sure all I had scrubbed the blood from under my fingernails.

Isaac smirked and kissed me gently. "Well, I thought of you too," he said. "We were at the home of Lord Mauldin and that annoying wife of his. They seem to think their daughter will be a good match for Edmund." He rolled his eyes.

I knew that his brother was Isaac's least favorite topic. I threw myself at him, kissing him with all the passion in my heart. I needed to forget what I had done. I needed to secure a future with him.

When we finally untangled ourselves from each other, I tried to articulately reveal my feelings. "Isaac," I said slowly.

"Yes, Violet?"

My name sounded heavenly when it came from his lips. "Why is it that your parents are so focused on getting Edmund married and ignoring you?"

"Oh, I'm sure once they get him tied down it will be my turn," Isaac shook his head. "Why?"

"Well," I bit my lip, unable to look him in the eye. "I just wondering what will become of us then."

Isaac hesitated, holding my hands in his. "Violet, I've never felt about a girl, the way I feel about you," he said, making my heart swell. "I don't know what the future has in store for us, and until just now, I hadn't given it much thought." He touched my chin and drew my eyes to his. "Trust me, they'll be working on Edmund for a while. I'm enjoying not being the center of attention."

"Why does everyone seem to doubt Edmund so much?" I sighed. "How are you so confident that our situation will go unnoticed for so long? Edmund could marry tomorrow – and then what?"

Isaac sighed. "Well, Edmund won't marry tomorrow, and I suspect that he will hold off as long as possible."

"Why?"

"Well, he prefers men."

"Yes, Judy already told me he prefers male Bloodletters. I don't see what that has to do with it."

"No," Isaac interrupted. "Edmund prefers men in all ways." He stumbled over his words, embarrassment tinging his cheeks. "My brother lies with men, the way that I lie with you."

"Do your parents know?" I asked, without judgment. I was unsure of how Royals felt about these things, but for the commoners, all forms of love were accepted.

"I believe they suspect, but it doesn't matter. If he were born anyone else, it would be fine. However, Edmund is the Crown Prince and as so is required to produce heirs, which is already a challenge as it is." He shook his head and sighed, leaning back against the sofa and letting my hands fall from his. "I pity his future wife."

I rubbed my arms through the fabric of my dress. I hadn't meant to turn the conversation to Edmund again, but yet here we were. "Why did they assign me to him if he refuses to drink my blood?"

"Using his male Bloodletter in public would only fuel the rumors." Isaac said. "My brother is nearing forty, and it's time for him to take his place in the family."

"Forty?" I repeated with surprise.

Isaac shrugged. "I'll be thirty this summer. Or did you forget about the Royals' longevity?"

The Prince didn't look much older than me. I was so used to being around him that I forgot that he was over ten years my senior and that he might live to be to two hundred. I held my hands tightly together on my lap. "Why are you doing this with me?"

Isaac raised his eyebrows. "Well, I thought that was obvious."

I needed to hear how he really felt. "Tell me."

"I love you, Violet." He leaned in and whispered against my ear.

Shivers rushed through my body. So, it was true. "Even though I'll grow old and die? Even though that if we were caught it would be the end of me? Even though one day your parents will force you to marry a woman you don't love in the name of politics?"

Prince Isaac pulled me to him and wrapped his arms around me. I settled into his strength, basking in the warmth that radiated from his body. "I don't want to think about that right now. Let's just enjoy this while we can."

I nodded and surrendered my body to lust for the second time that night.

I would not give up yet. I would find a way for us to be together.

I would find a way to become a Royal.

TWENTY-FIVE

A WEEK LATER I RECEIVED A REPLY FROM AMELIA. I opened the letter and was unsurprised to see her response. *How romantic.* She hadn't missed my hidden meaning at all – she had, however, failed to veil her response. I examined the envelope, and it looked like it hadn't been tampered with. I'd have to be more careful in the future.

When I looked at Isaac, I saw more than a handsome face and a well-read man. I saw an escape from this prison. A way to break free from being a Bloodletter. I could not sit by idly and wait for his brother to take an interest in my blood. I would not sit the days away in my room, only to be freed when he needed a companion for a social event.

I was Violet Ackerman. I had been raised to be more than just an accessory. My mother had raised me to be a Minister. I was just as well educated, well-mannered and well-spoken as these Royals. I could be one of them. I just needed to find out how to do it.

Prince Isaac was my door into that world.

The next night when I met him, I blamed women's problems and insisted that we read instead. It was easy to mask my intentions by asking to learn more about his great-grandfather. Isaac looked up to him more than his own father.

Isaac cracked open the massive volume of *THE ROYAL BLOODLINES*, which ended at the death of his great grandfather and featured a brief account of his father's coronation.

I pointed at the photo of his father, King Luther. "That's going to be your brother one day, trussed up like that." The formal outfits for the coronations were heavy with fur and jewels, as it was a tradition to hold them around the Winter Festival, no matter when the predecessor died.

Isaac's lips pressed together. "Yes."

I looked up at him. I had meant for the snide comment to be more of a joke. I leaned back against the chair, tapping my fingers on the mahogany table we shared. "What's wrong?"

Isaac shrugged and turned the page.

I could tell something was bothering him. "Come on, you can tell me. What's wrong? It's not because we couldn't… y'know,"

"No, no. Not that," Isaac insisted with a laugh. "I'm not that kind of guy." He looked down at the article that recounted the coronation. "I was just thinking how I would have liked to be there." He paused. "And wondering what Edmund's coronation will look like."

Isaac's face was easy to read. "Do you not think he'll make a good king?"

Isaac sucked in a breath. Obviously, he had never said so out loud. Just thinking thoughts like that would be traitorous. He cleared his throat. "I never said that. I remember that when we were younger, he never much cared for it. He slacked during our studies and only did that bare minimum to get by. He hates social events and now that our parents are pressuring him to get married, well, you know how that's going."

I nodded. "The weight that an heir must bear is terrible."

Isaac looked up from the book and studied me for a moment. "You say that with such conviction," he said. "You never told me where you came from. How someone as well educated as you became a Bloodletter."

The gentleness of his inquiry shocked me. He was right, every time he asked, I changed the subject. Not even Lady Carrol knew where I was from. It was a secret that was held by Madam Desjardins fiercely and with good reason. If a Minister was giving his child away to be a Bloodletter, surely that would cause some sort of uproar between the commoners. Especially when the fictitious story of my death had already circulated the newspapers.

Isaac noticed my hesitation. "You don't have to tell me, Violet. I'm just curious; it keeps me up at night," He said, choosing his next words carefully. "Most Bloodletters that come here have to go through rigorous etiquette training. Most of them don't even know how to read. Their situations were thrust upon them in dire circumstances and I always feel sorry for them. You, you're different."

My chest tightened with emotion. If I couldn't trust Isaac with my secret, who could I trust? "Ok," I let out a trembling breath. "My name is Violet Ackerman." I didn't stop when his eyebrows shot up in surprise. "I was supposed to be the heir, the eldest of three children. When my mother died, my father sold me to a Blood House in Afonyr and that's how I was entered into the Collection and came here. I wasn't even eligible yet, but because of the lack of Bloodletters to choose from, I had to stay even though a year hadn't passed."

Isaac was silent, taking it all in.

"My mother died in April." I said, and that was when it hit me. She hadn't even been gone for a year. I had been sent to the Blood House shortly after and it had overturned my entire world. If the girl I was a year ago could see me now, she would have wept for me. I stared at my hands. "I hadn't realized how little time has passed," I admitted.

The ticking of the clock was maddening. I waited for Isaac to say something, anything, to get my mind off what had happened to me.

"I'm sorry, Violet," he said finally. "Truly, I am." He rose from his chair and kneeled beside me, holding my hands tightly. "Now I see why you are the way you are."

"And what way is that?"

"Amazing." Isaac kissed my cheek. "You deserve more than this."

I chuckled and blinked away a tear that had been lingering in my eye. "You're right and I believe this was the way I was supposed to realize my potential."

"What do you mean?"

"My mother raised me to be the perfect lady. She had big dreams for me. There was no doubt in her mind that I would succeed my father and become the Minister of Wythtir. However, now I think I was meant for something more." I met his gaze.

Isaac smiled, making my heart squeeze tighter. "If it's any consolation for your pain, I'm glad that I met you," He paused. "I love you more that any girl I've ever known, even though it's forbidden. You're so much more to me than just a Bloodletter."

I couldn't help but blush.

"I was thinking about what you said last week," Isaac continued. He pulled up a chair and sat beside me. His fingers brushed my arm.

I glanced down quickly to make sure the scabs had vanished. I knew they had, but I couldn't get the image from my mind. I swallowed and forced my attention back to him. "What about it?"

"Well, you seemed quite pessimistic about the possible outcomes of our relationship," Isaac sighed. "And with good reason. I've tried not to think about it, but I cannot just keep putting it off. One day someone will discover us, no matter what we do and when that day comes, I want to be prepared."

"There's only one way that this won't end badly."

"How's that?" The Prince asked.

I leaned over the table and found the book I had been reading from earlier. *A Complete History of Bloodletting*. "In here." I flipped to the folded page and pointed to the circled passage.

"Oh, you've been reading this one too." Isaac's cheeks reddened slightly. "I don't know." He said softly and shook his head. "It's never been done."

I tightened my grip on the book in my hands. "Just because it's never been done doesn't mean it's not possible," I insisted.

"Become Royal, Violet? Do you have any idea how much risk there is? No one ever lived through those experiments."

"I know. I read the chapter," I countered.

"Then why would you suggest it? You'll die! I don't want to lose you," He added softly.

I clenched my teeth. "One day I'll be lost if we do this or not. You said so yourself. We will be discovered. It's not a matter of if, but when." My stomach clenched at the thought of having to kill another person to guarantee our safety, but I would stop at nothing to be with him. "Becoming a Royal is the only way for us to be together."

Isaac slumped back in the chair and rubbed his temples. "What you're suggesting, Violet, is madness."

I stared at him in silence. I had made my decision, but I couldn't do it without his help. "Do you have any better ideas?"

"No," The Prince sighed. He rubbed his hand over his face and looked at me. "Violet, I love you, and I would do anything for you, but I can't risk your life."

"I see," My jaw tightened. "Well I guess then we won't be seeing each other anymore." I stood and closed the book.

"What? Why?"

"Just being here with you is risking my life," I said. "If we're discovered, you know that it will be the end of me. Best case scenario I'll be cast out. Worst case, well I need not imagine that."

Isaac bolted to his feet and pulled me against him. "Please don't be like this. We'll figure something out."

I stared at him steadily, not letting my doubts show. "Then make me a Royal, Isaac."

Isaac flinched, but his arms did not loosen. "If I promise to look into it more, talk to some people and see what I can find out, will that be enough for now?"

I considered his offer. "You'll look into what can be done for me?" I couldn't hide my hopeful tone.

"Yes, I promise," He said. "But you must promise me something in return."

"Of course."

"Don't do anything rash. I will solve this problem the best I can. In the meantime, I want you to be safe."

I nodded. "Alright, deal."

Isaac breathed a sigh of relief. He stroked my cheek and kissed me softly. "I love you, Violet. No matter what happens, I'll be yours."

I dropped the subject after that. There was no use. I would let him try to find an alternative, but I was determined to become a Royal. It was the only way for us to be together.

It was the only way that I could redeem myself.

TWENTY-SIX

HALFWAY INTO MARCH, I WAS GROWING IMPATIENT.

Spring was the time for parties, a ball or a dinner was held every night. The highest Royals had nothing better to spend their wealth on. As Edmund's personal Bloodletter, they expected me to attend them all.

The richest of the Royals could also employ their own Bloodletters and it was beginning to feel like a competition. Like some sort of obscene dog show, where the most beautiful, well-mannered, and best dressed Bloodletters would be out on display for all to see. Thankfully, because I belonged to the Prince, no one was permitted to taste my blood. But the others had to share with whoever took an interest in them.

One evening, I stood a few paces away from Edmund, just within earshot in case the Prince called for me. He had not taken blood from me yet, and I doubted he would start anytime soon. When I wandered too far, his mother often shot me unfriendly glances, so I had learned to stay within an acceptable range. I stood in a lilac-colored dress with my hands folded in front of me and my eyes to the floor.

The Saxons were being entertained by a family with three beautiful eligible daughters. They all had surrounded Edmund all evening and it was impossible to miss the boredom on his round face. My heart squeeze with pity for him. I had tried to console him occasionally, trying to sympathize with him over the pressures of an heir, but as he was ignorant of my past, always shrugged me off.

The Crown Prince's lack of motivation was infuriating. Prince Edmund was destined to be the king of Inwaed, one of the most powerful countries of all time. He would be the most influential person in the country; even though the best rulers always considered the opinions of the government, he would retain absolute control. He should be studying, making allies, finding a suitable bride – even if it were only for breeding purposes. But he just sat idly while the wolves began to circle.

Prince Isaac had been invited to this party as well. When the daughters grew tired of Edmund, they turned their attention to him. He was infinitely more charismatic than his older brother and reveled in the endless attention.

I held my hands together tightly, feeling my cheeks burn as I had to watch the trio of ladies drool over him.

Isaac played his part perfectly and tried to direct their attention back to his brother whenever possible. After dessert, the girls had abandoned Edmund all together.

My stomach growled, and I placed a hand at my navel. I would have to wait until we returned to the palace for food and rest. I shifted in my shoes and wiggled my toes, sending pins and needles up my legs. Soon the party would be over, then I could relax.

Isaac caught my eyes and sent me a small smile. With the nightly events, we could not spend as much time together. I missed him every night. I hung onto the hope that we would be able to find a way to be together soon. I quickly looked away in case someone was to notice.

I wanted to go home. I had not missed the way the man of the house kept eyeing me up and down like a piece of meat. I couldn't tell whether he was lusting after my body or my blood, but I was grateful when the night finally ended.

I rode home in a carriage with two of the other Bloodletters that served the Saxons. They never spoke to me. I was an outsider to them, being a personal Bloodletter. They were only staff. The King and Queen used their services occasionally, but they attended the events as a show of wealth and nothing more. The Royal couple has personal Bloodletters back at the palace, but their identities were unknown to me, even after all this time.

I supposed it had something to do with security, but I had never asked. I was the only personal Bloodletter who was paraded around at social events and I was sure it had something to do with squashing the rumors about the Crown Prince.

I stared into the night, watching the scenery go by as we hurried along behind the Saxon's carriage. A pair of armed riders flanked either side of us for security.

I pulled my shawl around my shoulders and shivered. There was a draft slipping through the door and it was not yet warm enough to be outdoors uncovered. I took a quick glance at the Bloodletters who shared my carriage.

One woman and one man. They both looked tired, weak, and cold. I remembered those days of constant Bloodletting and I did not envy them in the slightest. I didn't know their names, nor did I care to learn them, taking Judy's advice not to get attached. After all, we Bloodletters were delicate and short lived.

I would save myself. Even thought Isaac thought it was impossible. Even though the history books had barely any clues. I would find a way. I would not be like the rest.

∞

Books surrounded me when Isaac joined me the next night. My red dress pooled around me and I had heavy history books in my lap. *A Complete History of Bloodletting* topped the pile. Many books hinted at the science of Bloodletting and the experiments that had been done, but none told the whole picture. I flipped through multiple texts at once, writing notes on a paper that I kept hidden in my hair during the day.

"Good evening, darling," Isaac said as he took his familiar place across from me. He had an old book in his hand. He must have noticed my eager eyes and held it up. "I think I've found something."

I took the book from him, carefully cradling it in my hands. It was worn and brittle. I cracked it open where a ribbon had marked a page. It was a journal, not a printed book, it was something much more private.

"Where did you find this?" I whispered.

"My father's personal collection." Isaac replied with a paranoid glance around the empty library. "But there's something very important I need you to see." He pointed at a specific paragraph.

My chest grew tight as I read the passage.

Yesterday, my grandfather met with Dr. Coleman in an attempt to save my father's life. He said that a blood transfusion would necessary, but father was too weak. Dr. Coleman worked with my grandfather on many blood projects. My grandfather wants to go through with it anyway, but I'm not sure if I trust him. The doctor is rumored to have worked on experiments involving the blood of Commoners, which is how we got into this mess in the first place. I must hope for a miracle, or my father will be dead within a fortnight.

"My father wrote this when he was about my age." Isaac whispered. He reached over and turned the page. There was a copy of the official announcement of Isaac's grandfather's death, dated only a week later.

I was silent for a moment. "Dr. Coleman?"

Isaac nodded. "Yes, he's the only lead we have. If we can find him. If he's even still alive."

"Oh, he's alive." I met the Prince's gaze. "And I know exactly where to find him."

∞

We copied the important details, which there were few, and then Isaac went to return the book immediately. The last thing we needed now was to get caught.

Dr. Coleman was involved in the Bloodletting experiments? It didn't seem possible. He was old enough, and I knew nothing about him, but he was so kind to me when I was under the rule of Madam Desjardins. He didn't seem like a scheming scientist type.

It seemed like a lifetime ago now. The memories came back to me in a wave. I missed the smell of the polish that Roger used to clean the wood trim, the taste of Victor's cooking, and the friendly faces of Miss Prescott and Mr. McCray. I even missed Heather's stern lectures.

I missed everyone, but especially Amelia. I hadn't written to her about any of this, lest it get intercepted; that would be like signing my own death warrant.

I waited, so consumed in my memories of the Blood House until Isaac returned to the dark library. He sat beside me, kissed my cheek, and set official royal letterhead before us. "Alright," he said. "Let's get in touch with Dr. Coleman."

TWENTY-SEVEN

THE NEXT WEEK WAS PAINSTAKINGLY SLOW. I met with Isaac nightly in the library, hoping that we had received a response.

By the eighth night, I was losing hope. I sat curled up in my usual spot, looking out the window at the gardens that surrounded the palace.

Isaac was late; I had lost count of how many times I glanced at the clock above the library door. I rubbed my arms and forced myself to concentrate on the book in my lap, but I had nearly memorized everything there was printed about experiments with Royal blood. The information was limited, and I had absorbed every last drop.

Dr. Coleman was our only hope now.

I shut my eyes and leaned my forehead against the window. The moon was nearly full, bathing the gardens in a soft milky light. The sound of the library door opening jerked me out of the trance.

"Violet," Isaac grinned. He held up an open envelope victoriously. "Dr. Coleman wrote back! He's agreed to meet us."

I scrambled to hug Isaac. "Yes! I was beginning to lose hope."

Isaac held me tight and kissed the top of my head. "Never doubt me. I love you and I would burn this city of the ground if it meant getting a chance of being with you forever."

The letter was very vague due to the chance that it could be intercepted. The Royals had to be suspicious of everyone. There had been attempts at a coupe over the centuries, so almost everything was subject to search. Thankfully, the mail of the ruling family seemed to be an exception, but we wouldn't take any chances.

The next night we were to meet Dr. Coleman at the Saxon's stables, as far away from the palace as possible. Sneaking out of my room at night had become second nature, so I didn't even break a sweat.

I dressed in black, a long cloak protected my body from the evening chill that bit at my skin. I met Isaac in the library. He was already waiting for me when I closed the door quietly. Our eyes met, and I felt my cheeks redden. He was striking in all black.

I blinked and forced myself to focus. Now was not the time to get butterflies. This was our chance to get answers. If Dr. Coleman had even the smallest clue about how to get this to work, then Isaac and I wouldn't have to hide anymore.

"How are we going to sneak past the night guards?" I asked. There was always a guard posted at every exit day or night. The ruling family's security was top-notch.

Isaac grinned and my heart fluttered again. "Who said we were just going to walk out the door?"

He took my hand and led me to the furthest corner of the library. The built-in bookshelves stretched all the way to the ceiling. Isaac paused for a moment before pulling a few heavy volumes from a low shelf full of dusty books. He fumbled for a second and then a loud snap of a switch being turned filled the silence of the library. There was a rumble and a small section of the shelves turned outward, revealing a path tall and wide enough for one person.

I gasped.

Isaac looked over his shoulder at me as he replaced the books to hide the switch. "Neat huh?" he whispered. "Thankfully, all of my military training has made me privy to the alternate features of this palace." He stood and gestured to the narrow passageway. "After you, my lady."

I hesitated for only a moment before summoning my courage and entering the darkness. I could hear

Isaac's breath in my ear as we made our way down the long, straight tunnel. There were narrow stairs that twisted down. It felt as if the staircase would lead us down into the center of the world. I lost track of time. I followed the path, putting one step in front of the other, not knowing what would come next in the sheer blackness of it.

Finally, we stopped at a door.

"What next?" I whispered.

"Open it," Isaac urged. There was not enough room between our bodies and the wall for him to move around me.

I pushed on the door and after a few shoves it opened. Light spilled in and musty air filled my lungs. We were in a cellar, the stable cellar to be exact. It smelled like straw. It was warm and comforting in a way that reminded me of the stable back home in Wythtir.

"Perfect." Isaac closed the secret door behind us. To the untrained eye it would look like nothing, but wood piled against the wall. He seemed giddy. "I've always wanted to use one of these," he said with a laugh.

I couldn't help smiling, but I had to keep my mind on the task at hand. "Ok, let's meet Dr. Coleman. It's after midnight. He'll be waiting."

Isaac's expression sobered, and he nodded.

Dr. Coleman was exactly where he promised he would be. He stood against the back of the stable near the watering troughs, dressed in a long black jacket. The doctor looked up. His eyes flitted back and forth between Isaac and me. He let out a low laugh and shook his head. "I should have known it was you, Miss Violet."

I didn't miss the emotion in his voice. We had intentionally left my identity out of the letter. I couldn't risk him refusing because of me. Isaac was the Prince and so his word was much better at making demands than a simple Bloodletter.

"Yes." I looked at him evenly. "It's me. Good to see you again, doctor."

"Likewise," he said while adjusting his glasses. He drew in a long breath. "Well then, let's get to business."

I glanced at Isaac as he spoke. "Dr. Coleman, I contacted you because I found your name in my father's personal records. It came to my attention that you have knowledge about experiments involving Royal blood."

Dr. Coleman shook his head and laughed. "No need to be formal, your Highness. I know exactly why you wanted me here. You want me to make her," He tipped his head in my direction and a chill shot up my spine. "A Royal."

Silence. The sounds of crickets were deafening.

"How did you know?" I asked.

The doctor shrugged. "That's what everyone always wants when I get summoned in the middle of the night." There was a twinkle in his eye. 'There was a reason that this knowledge was stricken from the books; too many people would seek what you are asking right now. And well, we couldn't have that, could we?" He paused, seemingly distracted by a memory.

"So, it can be done?" Isaac's grip tightened on my hand. Our hearts were racing in unison.

Dr. Coleman nodded. "Yes, my boy, it can be done."

"But my grandfather," Isaac trailed off.

"Was too weak to have any blood transfusion be successful." Dr. Coleman replied with a shrug. "Besides, it was a different process than making someone a Royal. Your great-grandfather tried everything. I was his last chance, and I agreed. But I knew that the chances were slim. Blood is a very tricky thing, you see."

"Becoming a Royal is possible," I interjected to bring the topic back to focus. Isaac's grandfather was long gone. I was the one who was risking everything right now, and I needed to know the truth.

Dr. Coleman nodded.

"You've done it before?" I asked.

The doctor nodded again.

"And you'll do it for me."

He hesitated and sighed. "Miss Violet, the experiments were risky. I was a young and reckless doctor. The experimentation was banned, and all funding ceased. Only one test subject ever survived, and I haven't done it since."

"But there's a chance." I pressed.

"Yes," Dr. Coleman said after a moment. "There is a chance. It's slim, but there is a chance of survival."

I clutched Isaac's hand. "We have to do this!"

There was sadness reflected in his eyes. "But Violet, I don't want to lose you."

"I'm dead the moment they find out anyway," I argued. I tried to reason with him. "This is the only chance that we will have to be legitimately together. I thought that was what you wanted."

Isaac smiled and kissed me.

Dr. Coleman huffed where he stood, obviously not thrilled with the public display of affection.

"It is what I want," Isaac said after breaking away from our kiss. "I just don't want to lose you."

I had no reason to doubt him. "Then you need to trust me. Trust that I am strong enough to do this." Our eyes locked, and he gave me a steady nod.

"Alright," he said.

A wave of relief washed over me. I turned my attention back to Dr. Coleman. "When can it be done?"

Dr. Coleman opened his mouth to speak but was cut off.

"Hey who's out there?" A guard wielding a lantern and a sword appeared, silhouetted by the castle lights in the distance.

The doctor shrunk against the shadows. "I must not be seen," he hissed.

Isaac and I exchanged glances, and the Prince waved him off. "We will call for you." He said as the doctor made his escape.

"What do we do?" I whispered, holding tight to Isaac as the guard came closer.

The Prince kissed my cheek. "I will confront him. You take the secret path back to the library. I will meet you there." His eyes remained locked on mine for a second and then let go of my hand.

Isaac strode out of the shadows and waved at the guard with a smile in his voice. "Not to worry, just out for an evening stroll."

The guard seemed relieved. "Oh, your Highness, I was worried it might be an intruder."

Isaac laughed. "I would be capable of taking care of anyone who tried to harm me, rest assured."

I made my move when they turned to walk back towards the castle. I sidestepped around the corner and grabbed the side door. It opened with a creak.

"What was that?" The guard turned on his heel and held up the lantern.

I froze. I was caught in the light with nowhere to go. There was no getting out of this now. We were caught and they would surely put me to death for my love.

∞

I sat hugging my legs to my chest on the floor. I had been locked in my room for days. No one had come to see me except to deliver my meals.

Isaac had ordered them to stop, but even he was not powerful enough to overrule the will of the King. I hadn't seen him since I was ripped away from him and dragged up to my room. I screamed and banged on the door for hours until my voice gave out, but it was all in vain. No one answered.

There was nothing to do now but wait. I opened my eyes. It was night again; that made it three days since I had been locked away. I supposed I should be grateful to still be breathing at this point. My faith that Isaac would bargain with his father was the only thing keeping me alive.

There was a knock at the door. It opened and someone pushed a tray of dinner in before the door was tightly locked again. They kept the mealtimes sporadic, in an attempt to protect themselves from me thinking up an escape plan, no doubt. Lucky for them, I hadn't even tried. What would be the point? It would only solidify my guilt.

My stomach clenched at the smell of warm soup filled the room. I had refused lunch and now I was starving. Casting aside my pride, I crawled to the silver tray and breathed in the scent of soup and fresh bread. With no one around to judge me, I lifted the bowl of soup to my lips and drank directly.

I drained the bowl. I was wishing for more when something caught my interest. There was a small folded piece of paper underneath the bowl.

I furrowed my brow with curiosity and unfolded the paper. It was in Isaac's writing.

Dear Violet,

I hope you are not being mistreated. I have been forbidden to venture to the library or anywhere near the Bloodletters. My father is furious. I have admitted my love, but he is set in his ways. There is only one way that we can be together. You know that means. The plan is in motion. Wait for me, my love. All will be well.

Yours,

Isaac

The words were written tiny and neat in order to fit on such a small scrap of paper. I sighed and held it in my hands tightly. Warmth spread through me, filling with me with joy. Isaac wasn't going to give up on me. We would be ok. He would make me a Royal.

∞

The next morning there was a knock at the door. Instead of a tray of breakfast being unceremoniously shoved across the threshold, Judy appeared.

"Miss Violet," she chirped. The maid went about opening the blinds and laying out an outfit, as if it were any other normal day.

I groaned and buried my face in a pillow. For a moment I forgot that I was being kept a prisoner in my room. I bolted up. "Judy?" I gasped. "What are you doing here?"

Judy emerged from the bathroom. I could hear the roar of water and the promise of a bath. "Your audience has been requested," she replied. "A meeting with the King and Queen."

The momentary happiness was stolen away, and my mouth went dry. "Oh," I barely managed a whisper.

Judy's lips pressed into a line. I looked up at her from the cocoon of blankets I had buried myself in. "Ma'am, I know something troubling is happening." She gestured around us. "The walls have ears, you know. But I believe that the Prince will be there as well." She hinted, and it gave me hope.

I nodded. "Then I must meet them and look my best." If it were an audience with the Saxons or my executioner, I would be ready.

TWENTY-EIGHT

I ENTERED THE ROOM FLANKED BY TWO GUARDS.

I held my hands in front of myself stiffly and walked in small, controlled steps. At my request, Judy had abandoned the simple blouse and skirt that she had originally taken from my wardrobe and instead helped me into a magnificent purple day dress. My hair was pinned perfectly, and I did not let a shred of my fear show through.

One thing that I was taught during my days as a Minister's daughter was to never show weakness around politicians. The wrong move or glance could prove fatal. Literally fatal, in my case today.

King Luther and Queen Leona were seated at the front of the room. A long stretch of red carpet was between us. The guards walked me towards them slowly and ominously. The King's advisers were seated along the wall and whispering amongst themselves. I counted six men and two women. Standing beside the King was Isaac. Edmund was nowhere to be seen.

I stopped at the edge of the red carpet. I stole a moment's glance at Isaac, whose expression was unreadable, before returning my attention to the King and Queen. I stood silently, waiting for them to make the first move.

The King examined me carefully. "What is your name?" His voice was loud and commanding.

"Violet, sir," I replied. I did not give another word away.

"From which family?"

"That information is lost to me, Your Highness. I only have memory of the Blood House where I lived under the care of Madam Desjardins." I hoped he would not press further. My eyes flicked to the Queen, who was watching me carefully. There was a small spark of warmth in her eyes, but I didn't count on it saving me.

"Do you know why you were called here today?" The King continued.

I kept my hands tight at my sides. "No, sir."

The King chuckled and shook his head. "Are you sure about that, child?"

I hated his condescending tone. "Any answer I give would only be an educated guess, your Highness." I spoke with respect, not sarcasm.

There was a silence. Isaac cause my eye with a tiny nod. It gave me hope. We would emerge from this together.

The King's face was expressionless. The advisers were silent, watching us intently. I knew enough about the Royals to know that the advisers were little more than decoration for matters like this. Ultimately, my fate was in the King's hands.

"Violet," he said. The King's voice echoed in the room. "You were found on the palace grounds past midnight four days ago. Prince Isaac has admitted that you were together when this happened. He has also admitted to an unapproved relationship with you." He paused. "Violet, you are the personal Bloodletter of the Crown Prince Edmund. As such you have the strict responsibility for your actions and to protect the purity of your blood at all costs."

I nodded, waiting for him to continue.

"Do you admit that you were meeting Isaac that night and that you put your blood purity at risk?"

"I was with Isaac," I replied. I had done nothing to harm myself and I would not admit to *dirtying* my blood. Edmund wanted nothing to do with me anyway and the King and Queen knew that.

"Are you aware that this is a treasonous act against the Crown Prince?"

My confidence faltered. "Treason?"

Isaac stiffened. "Father," He was cut off as the King raised his hand for silence.

I bit my lip, waiting for the king to continue. His words were weighing on me heavily now. How was I going to get out of this? I glanced over at Isaac.

"Violet, if you admit to this, you will be stripped of your status as a Bloodletter and executed for your crimes against the House of Strix," The King said.

My throat prickled with dread. I tried my best to keep hold of my composure. What was Isaac waiting for? Wasn't he going to save me? I stuttered as I replied to the King. "Your Highness, I did not put my blood in danger and thus did not endanger the Prince. I had no ill intentions towards your family."

The Queen eased back in her chair and whispered something to her husband. They exchanged knowing glances, and the King turned his attention to Isaac.

"Prince Isaac," he said. His voice was all business. There was no hint of affection for his second son. "Do you admit to being on the palace grounds after curfew with this young woman?"

Isaac nodded. "Yes, I do, Father." His eyes locked on mine as he admitted the truth before the King and Queen. "*I love her.*"

There was a collective gasp from the advisers. One frail older man nearly fell off his chair. They huddled together in a frantic whisper.

"Silence!" the King shouted.

I swallowed hard, waiting for him to speak. I balled my hands into fists to hide the trembling. It was nearly impossible to conceal my nervousness now. This was not how it was supposed to be. I was supposed to become a Royal and be welcomed with open arms. I was no traitor.

"Your love for her will be her death." The King rose from his chair. "She will be executed tomorrow morning."

"No, please," Isaac pleaded with his father. "Father. Your Highness." He fought to find the right words. "I love her. There has to be another way."

"You betrayed your own brother, Isaac. You should be grateful I am sparing your punishment as well." The King's words were like ice. He looked at me and waved dismissively. "Take her away."

∞

I was stripped of my fine clothes and dressed in a scratchy cotton dress. I was in a storage cell in the palace's basement. The other holding cell was empty, and the floor was damp but mercifully clean. I sat in the corner with my knees to my chest. I had not cried a tear.

There was nothing but sounds of dripping water and the smell of wet stone to comfort me. I would have never predicted that my last day would have turned out like this. I counted the moments until I would hear the door open and be led to the executioner's block.

I was woken from a restless sleep by the sound of the heavy wooden door scraping against the stone floor. I tensed, hearing not one but three sets of footsteps. My stomach clenched, and I glanced around for a clue, something to help me make a break for it when they opened the cell, but there was nothing.

The footsteps stopped the cell door. I looked up, unable to believe what I saw.

Queen Leona was standing there, looking out of place in her velvet gown and shimmering pearls. She smiled at me. I must have been hallucinating.

She spoke. "Good evening, Violet." Her voice was warm and caring. While I had been near her on many occasions, she had never noticed me or spoken to me directly before.

My heart was pounding in my chest. "Good evening, your Highness."

Queen Leona's smile widened, and she let out an airy laugh. "You have impeccable manners, even when dressed in a sack." She motioned beside her and the other two people came into the light. Dr. Coleman and Prince Isaac.

My mouth fell open. On one hand, it embarrassed me for Isaac to see me dressed like this in a damp cell, but on the other hand, my heart was bursting with joy. I struggled to my feet and my hands clasped around his through the metal bars. "Isaac!" I sobbed. "I thought I would never see you again."

"I wouldn't let you down, my dear," he said. "I just needed time to make a plan."

"What plan?" I wiped tears from my eyes.

The Queen patted Isaac's shoulder. "My son tells me you are his true love. His love goes beyond your blood and to your soul. The King is not romantic, but I realize now that if Isaac has found his love, then how can I deny him?"

My heart fluttered.

"My mother wanted to test your faith," Isaac added.

"You proved today that you would die for your love. That is something that few people - Royal or Commoner - would not do." The Queen said. She stepped back and motioned to Dr. Coleman. "I have tried to reason with my husband the King. But, in order to save your life, we all know what must happen."

I nodded. "I'll do anything."

TWENTY-NINE

SILENCE WEIGHED HEAVY IN THE ROOM. The Queen and the doctor left to prepare everything for the blood transfusion. They left Isaac and me alone.

I wrapped my arms around myself in shame. I hated the Prince seeing me like this - vulnerable, cold, hungry and dressed like a pauper. I didn't even bother to brush the hair from my face; it would do no good.

The Prince was not put off by my appearance. He wrapped his arms around me and smoothed my tangled curls. "It's going to be ok, Violet."

I surrendered my last ounce of strength and fell against him. I would not cry, I would not complain, but inside I was terrified.

"I know you're scared," Isaac said, as if reading my mind. "I am too." He admitted with a chuckle. "But it's going to be alright. I have faith that if there is anyone strong enough to complete this transfusion, it's you. Fate would not have brought us together otherwise."

I nodded.

Isaac lifted my chin, and we locked eyes. "You're beautiful, strong, intelligent, everything I could have ever hoped for."

Our lips met in a feverish kiss.

"I wish it didn't have to be this way," I said when we pulled away.

Isaac nodded. "Me too, I wish I could have you just as you are," he agreed. "But that would never work. You'd grow old and I would have to live on without you." He clenched his teeth at the thought. "I'm just sad that I'll never be able to have your sweet blood again."

Royal blood was deadly to other Royals.

My heart skipped. "Do you want one last taste?" I asked, my voice barely above a whisper.

The Prince's eyes widened. "Are you sure?"

I nodded. "Yes."

I had never been so sure of something in my life. If sharing my blood one last time would strengthen our bond and prove my love for him, then it was the only option.

Isaac hesitated only a second, his eyes flicking to mine and then down the veins hiding under my pale skin. He bit into the soft skin of my inner arm.

The heat ripped through my body like a deadly fever. There was no pain, only pleasure. Drinking directly from the body had been banned for so long; the modern Royals saw it as a way to spread disease and taboo. Isaac and I had something special. Taking my blood released an animal in him that I was only too happy to please.

The bond was indescribable. Our hearts raced as one and our spirits entwined themselves in this long-forgotten ritual.

Isaac broke away with a low moan. He was breathing hard and his pupils were dilated. "I know I've said it a million times, Violet, but you are delicious."

I smiled and used my thumb to wipe away a spot of blood for the corner of his mouth. I took a deep breath and then said the words I had been waiting so long to hear. "Alright, let's go make you a Royal."

∞

A room had been prepared for the medical procedure. We would have to move quickly, as my execution was scheduled that morning. The Queen's plan was simple: once I was a Royal, the King would have to accept me. She was sure of it. I had no choice but to put my trust in her.

I was given a rough, scalding bath and dressed in a clean white robe. The room had been scrubbed spotless and was empty aside from a bed and various medical tools. Dr. Coleman mumbled as he made sure everything was just right. His nervousness was palatable; I had never seen him like this before.

I stood at the doorway with my eyes flicking back and forth. The medical tools gleamed in the light and the sterile smell made me choke. I let out a shuddering sigh.

Isaac placed his hand gently on my shoulder. "You'll be ok." There wasn't a hint of doubt in his voice.

I looked into his emerald eyes and kissed him softly. "Isaac, if I don't make it."

"No," He cut me off. "I don't want to even hear it. You will make it. You have to." He held me tightly. "I promise. If anyone is strong enough to endure this, it's you."

The doctor cleared his throat. "Come on lovebirds, enough of that. Let's get this done before sunrise."

It took all my willpower to let Isaac go. "So, you promise you've done this successfully, doctor?" I knew the answer, but I needed to hear it again.

Dr. Coleman nodded. "Once."

That wasn't reassuring, but it was a glimmer of hope in the dark pool of my impending death. "Alright. I trust you."

I followed the doctor's instructions. I was no stranger to having my blood taken, but this time it felt different. Part of me was glad that Dr. Coleman was here. I had been under his care for months; he knew my blood and veins better than anyone.

I laid down on the bed, exposed my arm and let out a deep sigh.

"Now this will take a few hours," The doctor said as he set up the contraption next to me. He glanced at Isaac. "Your highness, if you would." He gestured to the chair beside me.

The prince took his seat and exposed his arm closest to mine.

Before I could question it, Dr. Coleman offered an explanation. "The transfusion needs to be done with strong, pure Royal blood. The Prince here is the best candidate out of any of us. We will fuse your blood together and," He paused. "If all goes well, your body will accept the blood."

My heart was pounding in my chest. I watched the shining needle in the doctor's hand and bit my lip.

Dr. Coleman smiled. "Trust me, Violet. This will be unpleasant, but I will do everything in my power to keep you safe."

Without warning, the needle jabbed into my skin and I flinched. The gauge was large, wide enough to let blood flow freely. He jabbed my other arm was jabbed next. One would drain me of my common blood and the other would infuse me with Isaac's Royal blood.

The doctor then hooked Isaac up to the other side.

My heart pounded harder. This was it. This is what I had been waiting for since Heather gave me the brief sliver of hope. Now all I had to do was not die.

Easier said than done.

I swallowed hard trying to get rid of the lump in my throat. I hoped that I looked calmer than how I was feeling inside. I had to be strong and focused or else I would die tonight. I closed my eyes and relaxed my head on the pillow.

"Alright," the doctor said. I heard him clap his hands together. "Let us begin."

At first there was nothing but a brief twinge in my arms as he let the clamps go and the blood transfusion began. I took deep breaths, counting the seconds and attempting to calm my racing heart as Heather had taught me to do when bloodletting. Being nervous would only make the blood flow faster and put me at risk.

I grimaced as a wave of nausea fell over me. My eyes flickered open, but shadows dotted my vision. The blood was coming fast. My body began to grow cold and my fingertips twitched.

It was happening. Either I would die, or I would be a Royal.

The doctor released the clamp that was connecting Isaac's blood to mine. I knew the moment when it hit me because it set my body on fire. My nerves screamed as his blood entered my veins. I broke out in a sudden sweat and gasped for air.

"Keep still Violet." The doctor commanded.

I felt his hands on my shoulders to keep me from writhing on the bed and pulling the needles loose.

"Keep still. This will all be over soon." Dr. Coleman hissed.

My veins burned a map of agony throughout my body and to my heart. My eyes snapped open again for a moment before I was lost to the darkness.

∞

Violet.

I knew that voice. Where was it coming from? Who was it? Why did it sound so familiar? All I could see was darkness.

Violet!

A bright light flashed across my eyes. Was it the light from the procedure room? Where was I? I felt as if I were floating.

Violet!

That voice again. More lights.

All of a sudden it hit me. Memories came back in a rush. I knew that voice - it was my favorite voice in the world. The first voice I had heard from within the womb, the voice that told me bedtime stories, the voice that comforted me when I was hurting, the voice that promised me I was destined to be greater than I could have ever imagined.

"Mother!" I screamed out. Tears filled my eyes. I could hear her, but I couldn't see her. "Mother, where are you?"

"I am here with you," Her voice replied. "And I am with the Gods."

"Mother," I choked. "I miss you so much." I wanted to see her and hug her and never let her go.

"It is not your time yet, my dear daughter. You are destined for more." Her voice twinkled with a small laugh. "You are my most precious love, Violet. I'm sorry for leaving you. But you cannot join me."

My heart ached. "But, Mother," I whispered.

"Go back to him," she said. I knew she was talking about Isaac. "His people will need you more than you know. Go, child. Go and be the woman I always knew you would be."

THIRTY

WHEN I WOKE UP, I WAS IN A STRANGE ROOM.

The bed was enormous; I was nestled in plush pillows and warm blankets. It was not my bedroom I had grown accustom to as a Bloodletter. It was immaculate. I was in a room meant for a Royal.

With a trembling hand, I touched my face and ran my fingers through my hair. I was alive. Did that mean it was a success? Strangely, I didn't feel much different. In fact, I felt weak, tired, and driven by some strange thirst.

There was a knock at the door. I flung myself back against the pillows and shut my eyes tightly.

"Father, it's true!" Isaac's voice and two sets of footsteps echoed in the room.

"She is a Royal?" The King asked in disbelief. "This can't be!"

More sounds. Heels clicking on the floor. "Yes, my dear. She has become a Royal to prove her love for Isaac and to declare her dedication to Inwaed." The Queen's voice was soft and steady.

I kept my back towards them, and my eyes closed. They thought I was asleep.

"This is unbelievable." The King raised his voice and was shushed gently by the Queen.

"It is a miracle, Father," Isaac insisted. "Please, give her a chance."

The King made a low sound of begrudging agreement and then stomped out of the room with the Queen following behind.

I opened my eyes again and lifted my head from the pillows.

Isaac was standing there with his hands in his pockets and a boyish grin. "You're awake."

I smiled at him and attempted to sit up. Nausea crept up my body and I collapsed back down.

"Whoa!" The Prince rushed to my side. He sat on the edge of the bed and held my hands in his. "Take it easy, darling. You've been through a lot. Just rest." He leaned down to kiss me.

My lips were dry and cracked. I flinched away, and he kissed my cheek instead. "How long have I been asleep?" I asked.

Isaac paused to think. "About two days. The doctor has been in to check on you and he says you're doing really well." He grinned. "We did it, Violet. Now we can be together for the next hundred years and beyond."

I clenched his hand tightly. One hundred years was unfathomable to me. My stomach clenched with the fear of the unknown. Spots of light appeared in my vision. "Yes," I breathed as I blinked away the spots. "Isaac, I," Words weren't enough to express my feelings. My lover had not only saved my life but had defied the odds to ensure that we would be together despite everything.

I looked down at the intricately embroidered bedspread. "Thank you." I whispered.

Isaac pulled me into his arms. "Anything for you, my love."

I closed my eyes and rested against his shoulder.

We sat in silence until the peace was broken by another knock at the door. The doctor entered; he seemed surprised to see me awake. "Ah, Violet, you're awake. Doing much better I see." His eyes twinkled with pride. "The transfusion was an outstanding success."

I let him inspect me. The wounds from the needles had nearly disappeared. He checked my pulse, blood pressure, reflexes and senses. I was still weak and groggy, but he seemed pleased with my progress.

"Now that you've come to, it is important that we get some blood in you." The doctor said as he packed away his tools. "The next few days will be crucial."

Blood.

I would have to drink blood to sustain my powers, longevity, strength, and beauty. I swallowed hard. "Yes," I agreed. "I've had a terrible, indescribable thirst since I woke up."

Both the Prince and the doctor gave me a knowing look. The need for blood bonded all the Royals. The source of their power and the backbone of their identities was the blood of the commoners.

Dr. Coleman called for a servant to fetch one of the palace's Bloodletters.

Isaac stayed with me, wrapping me in a silk robe and helping me comb the tangles out of my hair. I washed my face and chewed mint and ginger to calm my stomach. I drank water, but it did not relieve the feeling of thirst for blood.

Lady Carrol arrived with a female Bloodletter who I did not recognize. I was suddenly thankful for the secrecy and isolation of the Bloodletter's wing. It would be easier taking from someone I did not know.

Lady Carrol stood at the threshold, her eyes wide as she looked me up and down. Her lips pressed together and then opened several times as if she wanted to say something but had lost the words.

Isaac strode over to her and whispered something in her ear. They exchanged glances and Lady Carrol bowed her head in submission. She was yet another person who knew our secret who would have to stay silent.

The Bloodletter was a woman of small stature with chestnut brown hair. She was dressed in a modest but well-made dress. I didn't think she could have been more than a year or two older than me. She walked and held herself with grace and purpose. In a word, well-trained.

I watched in quiet anticipation as the Bloodletter prepared. She set out her tools one by one and named them all in my head. I walked through the steps with her in my mind as if were standing beside her and it was my blood that was going to be drawn.

"Which arm, my Lady?" Her voice was soft.

It snapped me out of my trance. "Excuse me? What?"

"Which arm, my Lady?" She repeated.

I licked my bottom lip and looked back and forth from one arm to the other. "Uh, left." I said. During set up, I noticed she was right-handed, and her left arm would be easier and faster.

The Bloodletter nodded and with well-practiced precision drew a generous portion of blood. She handed it to me. "Here you are, I hope this pleases you." She was almost mechanical in her movements and words. She was experienced and obedient. Lady Carrol had trained her well.

My hands were unsteady as I took the small glass from her. I raised it to the light to watch the scarlet liquid swirl inside. The scent hit me, and my bottom lip trembled. I brought the delicate container to my mouth.

Out of the corner of my eye, I saw Prince Isaac give a reassuring nod. I could hear Lady Carrol hold her breath as I tipped back the glass and drank the blood.

Euphoria washed over me. The blood was delicious, and it satisfied my thirst. My entire body was buzzing with energy.

In that moment, I forgot about everything except the taste and feeding the fierce, God-like spirit that had blossomed within my heart.

∞

I stared out the window to the palace grounds below. The gardeners were tending to the tulips and the scent of Spring was heavy in the air. The sun peeked through the clouds and I watched the shadows grow longer as the afternoon turned to evening.

Everything was new. It was better, stronger, and vibrant. My eyes and ears were alert to the smallest movement or sound, and food tasted like it came from the gardens of the Gods. My strength returned and my senses continued to amaze me.

I was a Royal.

The doctor told me my heart stopped when I was on the bed. It was a miracle of science and faith that I had lived through the transfusion. Now, I was finally out of danger.

The doctor left last night under the cover of darkness to return to his regular life. We had been sworn to secrecy of his involvement with this ordeal.

The Queen had decided that no one but the family should ever know the truth of how I became a Royal. It would surely cause the commoners to riot. My new power had come at a price: a new life full of secrets. My past would be erased, and I would re-emerge as an esteemed member of the Royal Court.

I set aside the book on my lap and stood to examine myself in the full-length mirror. I wore a red gown with flowing tiers of chiffon. My blue veins stood out against my pale skin.

I looked different from the scared girl who was flung to the wolves by her own father. I had emerged from the flames of betrayal like a phoenix and rose higher than even I had thought possible. Here I stood as a Royal. A magnificent being whose power exceeded the average mortal.

Those who had doubted me would regret everything that they had done to wrong me. Now, with my newfound power and my Prince by my side, I would take back my dignity and punish anyone who opposed me.

It was time to settle the score.

EPILOGUE

I STARED OUT TO THE CROWD OF PEOPLE WHO HAD GATHERED OUTSIDE OF THE PALACE. Isaac held my hand with a tight, reassuring grip. I caught his glance out of the corner of my eye. He nodded to me.

I raised my hand to acknowledge the crowd, Royals from every level of the court had gathered to celebrate our wedding.

The feeling of dread crept up my spine. Would they find out I wasn't born a Royal? Would they shun me? Hate me? What would the commoners think? I had stolen the gift that should only be given by birth. I was artificial. Nothing but a ruse.

"Ladies and Gentlemen of the Court, may I present Lady Violet of House Saxon."

Violet's story continues in...

THE
BLOOD
CROWN

Coming Summer 2020

AUTHOR'S NOTE

Thank you for reading The Bloodletters!

If you liked The Bloodletters, please consider leaving a review on Amazon or Goodreads. This helps indie authors like me keep telling stories for readers like you!

If you're interested in getting news about upcoming releases, giveaways, book recommendations, and other great stuff, please consider subscribing to my newsletter!

NEWSLETTER: http://eepurl.com/gyMOwH

OTHER BOOKS BY SAMANTHA BELL

The Bloodletters Series

THE BLOODLETTERS (2019)
THE BLOOD CROWN (TBA 2020)

Psychic Academy Series

PSYCHIC SECRET (Psychic Academy 1)
PSYCHIC PRODIGY (Psychic Academy 1.5)
PSYCHIC LIES (Psychic Academy 2)
PSYCHIC TRUTH (Psychic Academy 3)

Stand Alone Novels
BECOMING HUMAN (2017)

ABOUT THE AUTHOR

SAMANTHA BELL is a writer, student, and self-diagnosed book hoarder. She has been living in her imagination as long as she can remember.

Support future projects by following Samantha Bell on social media!

FACEBOOK
https://www.facebook.com/samanthabellblog/

TWITTER
https://twitter.com/SamanthaWrites0

WEBSITE
http://www.samanthawrites.ca/

Made in the USA
Columbia, SC
20 June 2024